Rytius Records

Prince Kudu'Ra

New Dithyrambia Publishing, LLC

Cover design: Prince Kudu'Ra.
Cover art: Prince Kudu'Ra, *Fieldwork: Spirit* (2023).

First edition: September 2024

Kudu'Ra, Prince.
    Rytius Records / by Prince Kudu'Ra. –
1st New Dithyrambia Publishing ed.
    p.   cm.
    Includes illustrations.
    ISBN 979-8-218-51059-6
    1. Science fiction. I. Title

ISBN 979-8-218-51059-6

New Dithyrambia Publishing, LLC
PO Box 8899
Los Angeles, CA 90008
prince (at) newdithyrambia dot net

Acknowledgments

I would like to thank God, His Son Jesus Christ, my mother Saundra Taylor, her sister and my aunt Ama Shambulia, her son and my cousin Sundiata Shambulia, my grandmother Gaynelle Barksdale, her son and my uncle James Brooks, my great-uncle Lionel Taylor, my high-school debate coach Margo Kendrick, my high-school physics teacher Phyllis Catchings, my high-school guidance counselor Mary E. York, and my friends, who know who they are.

I would also like to thank my earthly though not biological father, the dearly departed retired LAPD Detective David Bludso, #14519, RIP; and my likewise dearly departed intellectual father, Loren Goldner, RIP.

I would like to thank those who danced prayers for me, and the many others whose names I do not know.

Dedication

This is for my son, Ise Kadiri Scypion Barksdale, future Magister Ludi, the very best of me and his mother, my daily inspiration, and the lovingest person I know.

Contents

Letter

Monday, February 4, 2143

Richus,

I make a tower of the errors of their ways to the glower of ours. U must help with records and books and all the truck u can muster. It will be to the greater glory and power of this principalitee and efforts here will be praised and rewarded. We have bilt two storys at the northest tip of Orange Mountain and there will be many more. In glower,

Your Master,

Feelharmonica

New Ark

The above were the contents of the letter delivered to Rytius on the Monday the freezing rains started to swell the Passaic. His ducks were lightly honking, the backyard brook was burbling, and he heard an urgent engine growl and cough from the kitchen where he was stirring groats and browning scrapple for his breakfast, so he dropped the spoon, removed the foods from their fires, and made his way quickly to the den, where he could retrieve the shotgun on the wall and post himself near the window, from which he could view his front porch safely from the side, and there he saw the prince's postman in face leathers and rabbit collar dismount his motorbike and, wrapped head to toe in wax hides over his denim shirt and trousers, run up on to the porch, drop something into the mail slot, and get just as quick away. He had delivered the letter to the wrong address, because on the envelope there was no address but only a single name, RICHUS, and only a township, EO, and neither the prince nor Ritius nor anyone peered among them concerned themselves with such low details as addresses, and either Richus or Ritius could serve as a proper misspelling of Rytius, if one knew that *y*s can sound like *i*s, and if one did not know that there were two of them and that they were brothers, and therefore that there must remain some distinction, and therefore that the strongest likeliest distinction between these two most similar names could only be the most striking subtlety.

Threat

He knew three things right away. The first was that the prince's tower of records had nothing to do with recordkeeping. The second was that the prince's tower threatened both his livelihood and his reason for being. The third was that he could waste no time redelivering the letter to his brother.

It was after sunrise, but not even halfway to noon. Rytius dressed lightly, throwing his shearling coat over his woolens as though he were going out to feed his ducks, resleeved and pocketed the letter, and stepped out into the drizzly icefall. It would be easy to redeliver the letter. House Coleman was on a short, quiet, dead-end street catercorner one of the largest apartment complexes in Eo, which contained the weightiest concentration of such structures in all of North New Jersey. Once a government-funded apartment project, an assisted-living facility for elders, a home for the afflicted, and then a hospice for the war wounded, it had long since lost all civic charter, and was now among Prince Feelharmonica's most productive residential properties. Ritius would be collecting rents from all the prince's apartment homes this week, and he always started here, near Brookside.

House Coleman

Rytius Records was Rytius's record store. But there were no prices on anything, and Rytius was interested in neither truck nor barter. He had never sold anything save his *Hardest* cider and duck eggs, and he had only occasionally traded anything at all. So it was more of a library than a store. Besides that, he had most recently traded man-about-town Tweety Bird Andrews a duplicate copy of the Partridge Family's eponymous 1970 debut album for a year's worth of *Gentleman's Quarterly* magazines (August 1995–August 1996). So it wasn't really about records, as in music, either. There was no lending. That never even crossed Rytius's mind.

Rytius both lived and kept shop in the home in which he and his brother Ritius chose their names. House Coleman was one of a handful of registered ancestral homes in the principality of New Ark, thanks mainly to the Colemans' long history of service to the princes of the realm. Ritius's shield was the fifth to adorn their gable. His pride was such that he often spoke of the exploits of his forebears and the beauty of the home they built, tempting both rivals and robbers to surveil the location, and would-be sycophants to call unannounced, which had only been a cause for embarrassment on Rytius's part. Of course no man dared to cross Ritius, let alone his master, the prince of New Ark, in an assault on their home. The only two who had attempted more than a stakeout at a respectable distance received two of Rytius's finest stilettos in their livers, simultaneously, while still in their vehicle—no easy feat.

◆ ◆ ◆

The Colemans were born warriors, tall, wide, and strong, and the people knew both brothers as warriors, more or less, not only from confusion but from the tale of their sudden orphanage and salutary recruitment into the service of Prince Appall, father of Prince Feelhar-monica, whom Ritius served as apprentice to his engineer, and whom Rytius served first as a messenger and later as apprentice to his scribe, transcribing dictated letters like this one, but better. Both brothers fought bravely for the prince during the Six Bridges War of 2137, most notably at the Battle of Stickel Bridge, successfully defending it and thereby the rest of County Essex against King Worrus Fish of New York, the greater power (by far) to the east.

Those two nobles had attempted for months to weigh the balance of, on the one hand, the tariffs and taxes levied by northern New Jersey on goods shipped across the six bridges connecting New York to northern New Jersey over against, on the other hand, control of Staten Island and thereby the growing illicit commerce, primarily out of Long Island, though many smugglers sail from south even of the Virginian Dominion. Trade had grown since the North Atlantic wars, then six years closed. In any case, the prince sent for his big brother Boy, who had made himself into the largest landowner in southern New Jersey—practically a Gardener himself by virtue of vocation and location, growing spinach and various squashes outside Princeton—to seek his counsel in these matters. The brothers schemed, the wives gossiped, the concubines grumbled, and Boy's eldest daughter Cheeda, 18, met well with Rytius, 20, by whom she was courted and loved, and to whom she promised to wed herself.

With his brother in his ear, it was not long before the perspicacious Prince Appall was able to place himself in the mind of the King of New York, and to conclude that what New York most needed was a peacable and stable buffer zone between himself and the mighty Virginian Dominion, the great power to the South. Appall's principality, comprising most of northern New Jersey and extending down to Trenton, could be that very zone. In the same moment he understood how it was no accident that the tri-state region had enjoyed relative peace since the North Atlantic Wars. It was precisely because the King of New York had lost his navy and air force to the French that he now required protection from regional rivals.

While Prince Appall suffered no illusions regarding his military strength, he had quite acutely adjudged his strategic importance. Even before New York exploded the fragile peace it had managed to impose throughout the region in a premature bid for global dominance, southern New Jersey had long been an unruly outland wracked by the strivings of obstreperous Illadelphians, ill-used and discontented Gardeners subject to whomever's tax and requisition schemes, and land-seeking Dominionist settlers, one against the other, a difficulty for either kingdom—New York or Virginia—to manage. Either would pay dearly for its pacification, but Prince Appall already had his hand in one pocket.

So he invaded Staten Island first to communicate his strategy to King Fish of New York, and to remind him of his material priorities. Consider that tariffs and taxes are constant proportional costs, whereas the smugglers' coves of Staten Island—unknown in depth and extent— were a growing source of potential revenue, if properly regulated. Appall planned to return Staten Island in exchange for a greater share of the revenue, yes, but also for a deeper partnership where the Dominion was concerned: southern New Jersey. Appall took the King to war for the King's own sake, and even that of the King's rival to the south; Appall crossed swords with his benefactor, the better to protect his benefactor's table—the table off which Appall swept revenue into his own coffers— and, moreover, to afford that benefactor the material margin of safety he required. Appall shed New Ark blood to thrust himself between New York and the Virginian Dominion, thereby tasking himself with both their battles against the smugglers, thieves, bandits, and assorted revolu- tionaries of southern New Jersey, and simultaneously setting himself up to take the first blow in any conflict between the two powers.

That first blow came from the Virginian Dominion and landed heav- ily, surprising observers with its apparent senselessness. Boy's caravan was intercepted by what was only later deduced to have been a squad of Illadelphian mercenaries, who accompanied Boy and his family to their home outside Princeton, where they painted the walls with the yellow herpeton of the Gardeners, and left a list of locations at which the head matching each body would be found.

It was not until Prince Appall received Cheeda's letter from under house arrest in Baltimore that he understood the Dominion as New York did. He did not take as long to learn to hate them. It was the Dominion's position that it and northern New Jersey together could easily pacify southern New Jersey and win more favorable terms of trade with New York. The Dominion wanted the deal that Appall had already struck with New York.

Appall remained undeterred. The Dominion had killed his brother's entire family, but for his niece, merely to open negotiations against New York by threatening him with the very chaos he was already determined to quell. It didn't care for the peace Appall pledged to bring. It wanted the glower as well. Appall burned the letter and let his staff know that his niece had been spared, and that her life hung in the balance, but not that New York was innocent of the entire affair. That came out later.

The King of New York, meanwhile, refused the logic of Prince Appall's assault from Perth Amboy, and instead attempted to take New Ark directly from the east, via Stickel Bridge, where the full-hearted young Rytius, fighting for what he believed to be the life of his beloved in Baltimore, led his youthful squadron into doing precisely what was required of them, and more than anyone could have expected. Prince Appall took both brothers' oaths of loyalty and granted them their shields of service on that bridge that very night. New York regrouped and reattacked via Interstate 95, which was an even worse tactic; the King's men were repeatedly kettled and massacred between offramps and along the feeder roads as they deserted, and the surface streets either side of State Road 9, through the Ironbound district, ran with blood.

The Six Bridges War ended with the signing of the Covenant of New Ark and the establishment of the sovereignty of North New Jersey, of which Prince Appall became ruler, and which he set his sons to dividing among themselves. That warm winter the rains came early to melt the autumn snowpack in the Highlands, and those waters mingled overflowing south through the creeks, canals and rivers, baptizing the newborn New Ark in a flood. Prince Appall occupied himself that winter with the terms of Cheeda's marriage to the second prince of the Virginian Dominion, which sealed North New Jersey's limited agreement with that kingdom: Rytius's love being the price of their temporary alliance against the Illadelphians. That is when it became known that New York had nothing to do with the kidnapping and imprisonment of Appall's niece, Rytius's quondam bride-to-be. After the signing of their treaty, the King of the Virginian Dominion bragged that Appall's niece Cheeda had never been under house arrest, and he insulted his son, the second prince, by claiming that she was the better negotiator. As part of this humiliation of his son, he declared that Cheeda was the one who insisted on the lands around Princeton as part of the Dominion's settlement with New Ark. They included all of her father's lands, after all. Dominion let it be said that she was the architect of the entire affair, first setting her own price from House Coleman during her father's consultation with Appall, and then driving her own bargain hard in Baltimore. The heartbroken young Rytius left his service, and Prince Appall died of cholera some few years later.

The new King Hiram Fish of New York still licks his wounds for his father's sake, and for good reason. New York is rich in industry, agriculture, cuisine, language, arts, literature and music of all kinds, as it is filled with people of every nation, and it is accorded prestige and renown as it was in the olden days. It is the greatest of the northeastern kingdoms—greater than all those of Old New England, and of course that small sovereignty of North New Jersey—but it remains unable to project its power either south or west of the Bay of New Ark. Though not made of paper, the tiger is caged.

◆ ◆ ◆

But the people knew Rytius as a recordkeeper, as well, because of his listening parties, at which he and others would play music, read texts, display works of art, and share whatever stories their discoveries demanded.

There were listening parties before Rytius, but not like they became; he is said by many to have pioneered a game, an informal though unforgiving and ruthless form of presentation, judged by immediate acclaim or declaim of the gathered recordkeepers, wherein the presenter speaks and reads and plays in only the most interesting and exquisite combination of archaic locutions in their appropriate historical form, and only of matters arising from the material itself, which are also the sole topic of discussion. Anything said must arise strictly out of the material presented and make the most significant use of the most of it. This mode of presentation quickly became essential to any listening party, as participation was now a matter of critical judgment in which only the listeners' exquisite delight, surprise and insight could serve as the measure of success, while these joys were purchased with the vigilance with which recordkeepers guarded one another against improper inference. There are those who play a similar game without similar scruples, but the recordkeepers began to understand that their game had a logic of its own, another reason embedded in its deceptively simple form, which didn't require knowledge of its ends in order to be sustained by the joy it brought in the knowledge it built.

So Rytius was known beyond the battlefield, and not only in New Ark or even North New Jersey. He had heard of their sort of listening party even as far away as the southern coast of Baltimore Bay, near where Richmond used to be. This kept customers coming to his shop, and he reaped a sort of tribute, as those with treasures to be preserved often thought of Rytius first. He was, after a fashion, a wealthy man.

Tiara and Merrillee

It happened that Tiara was the early riser, and it had been that way since Atlantic City, and it was going on about twenty years since then. Merrillee wouldn't have it any other way, and let Tiara think what she wanted. That, also, had been that way since then. Merrillee was simply the better charmer, so she had to get up early anyway. She did try, but Tiara couldn't do it, and it wasn't because she was lazy or malingering. It was an actual matter of talent; a talent Merrillee would rather have done without. So she didn't like it, but she took her pleasure where she found it, and she found it in being better at something than high, mighty Princess Tiara, while Tiara never failed to remind her that her attitude, which should be gratitude, tended rather toward the tendentious and irritable, just as it had in Atlantic City, and no doubt before. No sooner did the Lord let her wake than she started in to grumbling, sowing dissension, and working iniquity. Merrillee let her 'buke, scorn and chastise, because Tiara didn't know just how patiently Merrillee had held her tongue these years since Atlantic City. Merrillee would never let her know, either.

Time was, Tiara loved to brag about the fame and fortune of her men, even before the money she got out of them, and Merrillee would listen graciously, with a smile on her face and a bottle of Give Me Your Money oil in her handbag. Next to the straight razor. Merrillee had used to joke that she was an *obey* woman, because her men did what they were told. She had had her own plans. Nowadays Merrillee told herself that she had been playing a longer game, and it was true—today. Time was, Merrillee had entertained her own fantasies of fame and fortune, and then vicarious fame and fortune, and she had had to set both of those aside, things being what they were. She could, however, wield power and might. That was true, today. In small ways.

She planned soon to tell Tiara that she had a new secret lover, and Tiara's precisely composed face would crack and fall off. Then she would tell Tiara that her new lover was a beautiful, well-admired and powerful woman, and Tiara's skin would turn green with envy. She might even pass out. God forbid she have a stroke. Meanwhile, it was among her dearest small pleasures to enjoy Tiara's performance of humility at Merrillee's expense.

It wasn't Merrillee's place to remind Tiara of what Tiara surely knew and must never forget, which was the simple fact that Merrillee had always been the rain maker, and she *still was*. And that was all that had ever mattered to either one of them. Merrillee therefore rested on her talent, and didn't let a word pass her lips. This morning. Things being what they were.

It would have been easier for them to split up in the morning, but neither wanted to be alone out there, in the pre-dawn darkness, under the Stickel Bridge overpass, nor exposed along the feeder road along the shore, or in those soft fields along the Passaic, where Merrillee did her best work.

So they stayed together, and Tiara came past Merrillee's small cottage daily every morning three hours before dawn, unlocked the door with her own set of keys, and refused to make tea for Merrillee but only made coffee for herself, and only on those days when Merrillee was not already awake. And that was usually the case, because Merrillee was often still asleep, and the gurgle of the percolator and the aroma of the coffee would wake her. She only ever made Merrillee's tea when the kettle was already on the boil. Tiara bought and brought her own better or worse coffee grounds from Cuba or Florida, via Staten Island. She stretched them with chicory or rye when she had to. Merrillee kept a cache of Earl Grey in a tin in the cupboard just above the percolator, between the BETTER BUSINESS candles and the Go Away Evil spray.

Tiara sometimes, not too often, turned her nose up and asked her her reason again for drinking tea instead of coffee like regular folks. She took pleasure in turning the tables on Merrillee, who she knew had always considered Tiara to be one of those precious, high-post, saditty bitches. She was just jealous, and always had been, because Tiara was what used to be known as high yellow, and she carried herself well. Merrillee was quite dark, descended from Jamaicans some time back, and she herself knew the tea to be an inherited Anglophilic affectation. She admitted as much, though she had come to enjoy the taste. Coffee had just gotten to be too harsh on her stomach sometime in Atlantic City. So a little Earl Grey with lemon and honey, or with milk and sugar, either one, depending. Tiara couldn't do much with such a response, and that's why she didn't bring it up often.

Tiara put them on a couple of eggs to boil as she sipped her coffee and went into her own thoughts in her own mind and Merrillee would take too long to pack her cart, knowing full well the night before exactly what she would need. An icy draft shot through the kitchenette every so often, and she told Merrillee that her tea was going to get cold if she took much longer, knowing full well exactly what they did every morning, and so each sip of her coffee was that much sweeter, her half of their shared morning ritual that much more exquisite. She would not reheat it but she would soon decant Merrillee's too-cool tea into one of two antique Thermos bottles for their trip to the shore. She would take her time, pouring slowly and cautiously, from high up above the bottle, so as not to waste one single chilly drop. She would fill the other with a freshly brewed cup of hot coffee. It wasn't a long trip, but it was cold, and while they were not old women, they were not young women anymore.

They carted and clattered their way down Central Avenue to the river. The rain was not yet hard and heavy, and the soil was not yet waterlogged. Merrillee found a spot between Division and Bridge, near some old railroad tracks. She unsheathed her wooden stake and rooping iron from their protective plastic scabbard mounted at an angle inside her grocery cart. The iron looked like a large rasp. In fact, it was a large rasp, teeth long worn down from years of rust and disuse. She laid her blanket down and stabbed the stake into the ground, as though it were the very heart of darkness. She drove it deeper, hammering it home with the flat iron. She began to stroke the head with the flat iron, as though she were filing it down. Back and forth, back and forth, at an angle here, or straight across there. She gestured to Tiara to prepare herself.

Tiara unhooked a hand-perforated bucket, a sort of custom sieve, from her own cart and was going to stand at the ready, but Merrillee was already snapping at her to get moving because nature was rising easy this morning. Tiara dropped swiftly to her knees, half on the blanket, half in the soil, to collect the worms that Merrillee had charmed out of the ground.

They were faster than one might expect, and they came out of the ground where they wanted, first there, then here, left, right, back, front. Merrillee stroked the head of the stake, grunting till Tiara's bucket was plumb full of juicy *Lumbricus terrestris*, common earthworms, the best for commercial food preparation. They don't taste the best—mealworms taste the best—but they're the best for the cost, which is often close to free. Tiara went to wash them in the river between two rinsing racks staked into the riverbed, and she plopped them into the cornmeal bucket.

By the time they made it to Brookside, the worms could have eaten, cleaned themselves, and dug and rooted around, if they liked. They would also be properly dusted for frying with a sweet or a savory spice mix. Merrillee's *Basic B*tch!* was the default option, with pepper, salt, and garlic and onion powder. It went well with eggs, diced onions, parsley and the like—any sort of savory breakfast food. Her *Sassy Lass* was more adventurous, and that had salt, pepper, allspice, a tiny bit of cumin or curry powder or both, garlic and onion powder, and cayenne pepper. Quite a bit more exotic, and Tiara did not like the curry with eggs, but many did.

Tiara preferred her own sweet mixes, and her favorite, *Gimme Some Sugar*, was brown sugar, cinnamon, allspice, black pepper and salt. She enjoyed this atop open-faced buttered toast. Of course, customers didn't care about that. They felt they were being cheated out of a slice of bread, and so it sold as a regular breakfast sandwich. *Honey Chile* was of course honey-based, with lemon juice, cayenne, and garlic. It didn't escape Tiara's notice that her sweet mixes contained savory, while the savory mixes stood alone. Tiara couldn't blame Merrillee for that. She wondered whether she could accept that as a fact of life. And whether it meant anything that she was on the mixed side of that fact of life.

Either way, business was good. It paid the rent and more besides. Their "Crispy Crawlers" Brookside Breakfast Buggy, serving the foot traffic between the market and the towers, was as good as any, and better than many sit-down establishments. Tiara didn't mind. Merrillee didn't mind. It was no Atlantic City, but neither was Atlantic City.

Special Delivery

Never hard to spot, Ritius emerged first from his black truck, before his guard, and even before his valet. He had the effect of a wedge in flowing water, tower residents scattering leftward into the towers and around corners further up the street, and shoppers streaming rightward, across the street, past the sentry gates, to disappear among the alcoves, stalls, and niches of the market. His shotgun swung out from under his oiled horsehide cloak and hit the side of the truck. Whereas the mere appearance of his armored black pickup truck emblazoned with Appall's red death harp insignia hadn't, this noise—halfway between the gong of a steel drum and the strike of a hammer on the head of a particularly large nail—alarmed the two women serving breakfast sandwiches from the BROOKSIDE BREAKFAST BUGGY.

They were cuckoo clock birds selling CRISPY CRAWLERS spiced in delicious combinations with eggs, toast, and various garnishes, precisely machined creatures of fine pattern and habit, clicking and turning in their appropriate grooves, reaching down here to pluck up the frying grease bottle, there to arrange the spice canisters along the edge of the cooktop, now to sweep and scrape the griddle, to hook spoons and ladles to hips, to tuck stray tufts of hair finally securely beneath their nets, and then to smile coldly at one another, the one wrapping one last sandwich for one last patron while the other began packing up. They had done this dance together daily for many years in several places and had never yet become friendly. It was between them and it was nobody else's business, but it was also as though the clock simply went into reverse, running the same actions backward, their setup now a teardown every bit as gear-driven but the action a bit more raggedy, with a little more rattle and shake. Ritius seemed not to notice them hustling off, stuffing soft supplies into the ripped, open mouths and swollen gullets of their overused rezippable plastic bags with ripped zippers, twisting them shut by twirling them in one hand, hooking the hoop to the proper peg poking out of the cart. They rolled out, busting up the group of tenant applicants they had been serving, cart wheels clattering against the cracks in the sidewalk, rattling around the corner.

Ritius stood tall, hitching up his six guns while his deputies formed his guard. He had always been contemptuous of bodyguards, and he doubted that these untested youth, even with their automatic rifles, would help much in a meaningful confrontation. There are doubtless many matters in which nothing can substitute for experience.

"RITIUS!" Rytius barked from across the street.

"RYTIUS!" Ritius hollered back. "WHAT'S GOING ON WITH YOU, BROTHER?"

Rytius crossed, smiling, leaning back, as he approached, as though he were awed and impressed with his brother's self-presentation. Ritius never acknowledged this disrespect. Rytius was the older brother, even if by only a year, and Ritius had often thought highly of his brother. He had always insisted that he named himself after his older brother. He had been a little confused about the different uses of *is* and *ys*, but he did mean to make his name like his brother's, and he did mean to make it different and mean different at the same time. Ritius would never acknowledge this disrespect, and he was sure that his brother would show no more.

"I received a letter for you today." Rytius raised his hands and opened his coat by the collar for frisking. The senior guardsman looked to Ritius for an indication. Was he really supposed to frisk this man, his master's brother?

Ritius looked cool and level at Rytius and wondered whether his brother was about to perform some slick new breed of impertinence. Ritius decided he wouldn't and frowned and shook his head. It would not be necessary to frisk his brother. There were still three automatic weapons aimed at his midsection in any case.

"You should deliver letters to our offices, brother," Ritius quipped, smiling broadly, as though to take the edge off. "If you want to be a postman, I am saying. Do it right, right?" He laughed in place of his guardsmen, who didn't dare. "Run up and get gunned up."

Rytius ignored all this dark admonishment and jocular assuagement and, perhaps to his detriment, put all consideration of the workings of Ritius's mind out of his own. He pulled the letter out of his jacket and handed it over. He was disappointed to find himself in the grip of a sudden and involuntary indecision whether he should suggest that Ritius read the letter now, because Ritius had forgotten so much since they were boys, and he likely had little cause any longer to read. Or then perhaps he should ask to leave before the letter were read, so as not to appear to play on Ritius's family feeling. Then he remembered that he didn't explain even the very first thing.

"It was delivered to the house this morning, and I opened it and read it, thinking it was for me," he said. Addressing the first thing delivered him from any difficulty managing his brother's reaction to the letter. That was entirely Ritius's responsibility now, to choose how to receive this letter, wrongly delivered, wrongly read.

Ritius opened and read the letter silently, lips unmoving. Rytius had underestimated his brother, and this mistake alerted him to the potential presence of others that he might have missed, because he had been underestimating his brother. Ritius's face was plain and Rytius could read nothing on it. When Ritius had finished, he folded the letter and pocketed it. He looked into his brother's eyes and asked him, simply, when it would be convenient for him to come by the store to do a proper inventory, so that the prince might know what treasures would fill his tower. Rytius answered that tomorrow Tuesday would be best, and the brothers parted with a pound.

Three Washerwomen

Once upon a time, long before New Ark's first flood, there were retaining walls along the two main riverstreams that flowed across it and into the rising Passaic. Called the Watsessing and Yantecaw rivers by those who lived there before, these tributaries were polluted, bound to commerce and exploitation, and renamed the Second and Third rivers. They were sources of food, then open sewers, then hindrances to real-estate development, then boosters of property values, then public trash receptacles, then protectorates of the administrative state and its environmental protection bureaucracy, and then everything changed. The walls decayed and crumbled into their streams, creating new and unexpected bodies of water, but also cutting off the free flow of fresh water through the city, and only Prince Appall undertook to clear the fresh waterways for the free use of the people, for which he was applauded and excused much of his ill treatment of them. Still, though the people had managed to maintain their own pipes and plumbing, the public waterworks—reservoirs, sewers, treatment facilities, storage—remained as they had been: inconsistent and unreliable in function and quality since before the North Atlantic wars. Water was Appall's only valuable public work, and his death by it must finally judge that work a failure.

But the rivers did flow, unhindered but for the occasional unlicensed homemade hydroelectric generator or bootleg grain mill, and so Rytius took a long way home through Soverel Park, to listen to the rush of the Watsessing there, and to check whether any wild fowl had yet returned, though he had brought nothing to feed them. The sky scattered crumbs of ice that melted upon contact with earth or anything therefrom, and the air hung on the knife's edge of actual cold, as though at any moment it might suddenly slice through your quickly donned scarf, and into your inadequately covered breast beneath to have caught you slipping. While the river walls had crumbled, the footbridges remained, and a half-dozen fishermen crowded Rytius's favorite, eager for a larger catch, hoping that the carp and bass would be agitated and disoriented by the rise in the waters. Three well-insulated washerwomen—they must have been in business, because it is hard to imagine a wife or concubine going out in such weather—were working in the stream, two on the eastern bank and one further up on the western bank, and they used the remains of the walls as shelves for their woven baskets of laundry, which this morning would not drain half dry during the work, but were taking an extended rinse from the freezing rain.

The first washerwoman was vexed behind this, because she had brought two extra-large baskets of clothes to wash on the eastern bank of the river, hoping to finish more work and receive more revenue that much more quickly, because the river's speed and depth would make the washing easier and more efficient, but she did not carry her thoughts to their conclusion. She had neither plastic sheeting nor oilcloth, and so the rain that made the river more powerful would also make her trip back more burdensome, because the water would soak steady through her laundry. Though light enough to work in—and she was clothed in full-body waxens and leathers—the steady drizzle accumulated within the fibers of her wash, and it was easy to imagine, were the temperature to drop just a bit, that the top layer of the laundry might freeze over and build up an icy surface, adding that much more weight. Rytius watched her quickly finish rinsing the last sheet of a set of bed linens on her portable folding rack, wring it out as best she could, pack it into one of her two gigantic baskets, fold her rack and pack it onto her back, and then undertake quite a bleak struggle to shoulder the beam on which her overweight baskets hung, one on each end. It was a sight to see, and the fishermen mocked her gently. "You got to get it square," "I don't know what you were thinking coming out here this morning," "You ain't got enough back to put in it," and talking about how it weighed near as much as she did. She could hardly get her footing there along the bank of the river, and she slipped and fell backward, whereupon each basket opened and some of the fresh wash of one fell into the mud and some of that of the other fell into the water and began to flow downstream. The fishermen fell to laughter and exhortations to hurry up and go get it, and Rytius chuckled and wondered what she would do and how she would do it. She yelped wordlessly and twisted out from under the beam and quickly dragged it a bit back up the riverbank, left the mudded items, and chased the ones in the water. A flotilla of undergarments—socks, drawers and T-shirts—moved quickly downstream, but also quite directly across, where they were caught in an eddy behind a pair of fallen branches. Her last-rinsed large sheet had escaped as well, swelled open like a sail and, most likely because of its length, overcame the small irregularities and cross currents to go smoothly downstream with the flow. The second washerwoman, on the western bank, was sympathetic, yelled "I got you, sweetie," and stepped in to retrieve those smaller items, while the first ran slipping and hopping distressed, a dozen yards downstream, past the third washerwoman, who laughed bitterly and could be moved no further, to get in front of the sheet, and she thanked Jesus that it caught itself squarely on the mouth of a large chain-link fish trap, so that the sheet was stretched long across the mouth of it, its lengths trailing in the water, and the flow of the water along the sheet was strong enough to pull the trap up, angling it up out of the water where it had been hidden.

The first washerwoman waded into the water to retrieve her sheet. Rytius watched her from the footbridge, and he appreciated that she didn't go to pulling and yanking immediately. She paused for inspection, so that she could remove the sheet with care. The trap was a metallic skeleton of a box, a sieve, but the sheet around it changed the flow of water through it. The water flapped the sheet in a rhythm against the sides of the trap, and that rhythm was also the constriction and dilation of the flow of water into the body of the box, which modulated less and more the flow of water out of the square links on top, which was visible as a pattern of rising and falling deeper and shallower ripples out of them, on the surface of the water. Whereas the section of sheet against the mouth of the trap was also a screen against the flow of water into it, and this plus the angle of rise protected those surface ripples from the agitation of the river itself, though it did not shape them. It let them be seen. Finally, a miracle of desecration, one section of sheet hung no more than 3 or 4 inches over the top of the mouth of the trap, and the waters rose unpredictably periodically to flap it against the top of the trap, scattering and scrambling the ripples entirely into a chaos out of which they formed again. It was an accidental device of crackpot ingenuity, designed for something else entirely. Rytius wanted to sketch it, but he had neither paper nor pencil, and it was too wet anyway.

"Don't come over here messing me up," the third washerwoman warned her even as she passed, returning to her station. "Hey, you did it!" one fisherman yelled. "Pure luck," from another. She stood discouraged over the pile of laundry that had fallen into the mud, and the second washerwoman yelled asking whether she wanted her to throw the smaller stuff across. The first washerwoman considered whether she could catch them in her already chilled hands, and she weighed the risk of them landing in the water or the mud. She considered walking across the footbridge, glancing quickly up at the crowd of men who had been mocking her, and so she crossed the river. The water had risen almost chest-high and it was a freezing rain, but she worked these waters daily, and she was well-insulated after all.

The Conflicts Constitutive of Historical Inquiry

Rytius's body woolens were damp and he was therefore chilled from his visit with his brother and his sojourn through the park, outside, in the rain, too lightly dressed. Water ran down his chest, stomach, neck, and back. He disrobed, there, just inside his door, drying himself with the thick undershirt. He walked himself and his damp clothes to the hearth in the family room. Last night's fire was long since out, ash-covered embers merely warm, and he did not have time to start another fire before he had to leave again. He draped his drawers across the cook crane, hung his undershirt on the pot hook, and padded into the dining room, where last night's dishes remained. He always cleaned his plate, but he didn't always clean his plates. The important thing was that last night's liquor bottle remained as well. He took a deep swig to warm his bones, thinking *blind Pharisee, first cleanse the inside of the cup so that the outside might also be clean.* He stood, waiting for the chemical warmth to spread throughout his belly, up his throat, the back of his neck, across the top of his skull, around his ears. He took fuzzy steps to get the gifts for the gathering, which is to say a full case of cider for the grown folks and an alphaphonics primer for the girl, because today was a very special day. His goddaughter was ready to choose her name.

7.1   Fila Green, the First Recordkeeper

St. Mark's remained a church. In 2108, the deacons, seeking protection from Prince Appall's tax collectors, leased the annex, in perpetuity, for a nominal rent, to one Polo Green, chaplain to the prince, who pleaded their case, pledged the nextborn male Green to the prince's service, and established the policy whereby churches may register their deeds to pay less tax. Polo died with one daughter, Prittiess, and when he came of age, her eldest son Fila inherited both the lease and the church registry concession. Pastor Snap Arnold, Polo's post-retirement appointee, took a liking to him immediately and practically adopted the boy, inviting him to family functions and introducing him as his son. He encouraged Fila to read widely, hoping eventually to guide him toward the ministry, like he did his nephew-in-law Erron, but Fila was a preternaturally independent young man with little care for his obligations either to the churches or to the prince, and he spent most of his time with friends from home seeking out, trading, and appraising the works of olden musicians when he should have been studying accounting or learning to plumb. He was released from the prince's guardianship and sent home, where he devoted himself more entirely to his passion, or according to lore and most of Fila's fellows, succumbed more thoroughly to his dissolution.

His collection consisted mostly of black and silver music albums, but soon also papers, books, and magazines of various languages, larger and smaller magnetic videotapes of myriad forgotten illegible formats, newspapers and clippings, reproductions, prints, and paintings of all media and any style, negatives, canisters, and albums of photographs both personal and journalistic, diaries, logbooks, daily planners, letters public and private, video silvers, comedy blacks, audiotapes of all sizes and systems, and assorted *petit objets d'art* soon overflowed the ample space available in the annex, and he busied himself with cataloguing and indexing them, and crafting synopses and commentaries.

He and his fellows had established a new sort of competition among themselves, not quite the game as it came to be, but finding and sharing the most stunning olden texts and artifacts, and the rivalry between Fila and his friend Tellem was particularly controversial. Whereas Fila was almost exclusively concerned with artistic and literary records, just as a matter of personal interest, Tellem became more interested in technological and economic records after discovering an old business and technology library while exploring the subway tunnels in midtown Manhattan.

Things were such that science in general—collective endeavor in pursuit of knowledge—had been on hold since before the North Atlantic Wars, given the harshness of New York's occupation, and it was the first time in years that anyone felt safe being in the tunnels for extended periods. Tellem's idea was that they should focus their efforts on these social sciences, which might provide helpful insights into what happened, how and why. In those days, when the game had barely taken shape and when what came to be known as recordkeeping was only just beginning,

Fila had no argument. He had only his own personal inclination, whereas Tellem had a mission and a purpose. Absolutely everyone agreed in principle with Tellem, even enthusiastically, but it turned out not to be a simple matter.

7.2   *Methodenstreit*

The first controversy was over whether Fila and Tellem were engaged in the same activity. It was clear to all that the activity was identical, only the object being different. Colloquially speaking, different subjects were investigated by different recordkeepers, but they were still keeping records.

The second controversy was more subtle, and it was whether the subject, philosophically speaking—i.e., the investigator—was changed by the material investigated. And secondarily, whether this change might meaningfully change the perception of the material, and thereby the function of the subject's methodology, so that two differently engaged subjects may eventually be said no longer to be engaged in the same activity.

It was Fila's insight that, where recordkeeping is concerned, the only activity is thought and the only object is knowledge. Surely, if those two concepts are useful at all, thought and knowledge must be universal. The various activities of minds engaged in the creation of knowledge ultimately cannot be different, because mind and knowledge are universal in their ambition, even if they proceed by contradiction and conflict, and even if this object demands that particular method.

Tellem's position was and has been no less compelling, perhaps because it is so familiar, particularly to those with his particular pragmatic bent: there is no use thinking or talking about universals before even approaching the object. One can never know whether one is ultimately right, and one will waste one's life in interminable arguments over finer and ever more abstruse debates over how one should approach. Meanwhile, so many particular concrete things can and have happened in human experience. There may be certain matters of something like abstract principle when it comes to things like basic human decency, as in the evil of murder, for instance, but trying to draw fundamental principles of scientific investigation from something like the dynamics of human thought cannot be reasonable, because the vast numbers of different humans think differently about different objects. Knowledge has nothing to do with conflict or controversy, but must prove itself adequate—as insight, revelation, advice, know-how, something that looks like recognition—to the real needs of our real existing lives, and we must be able to grasp it with our real existing understanding. All that we can say is the same as all that we can do: develop our principles from observing what works and our knowledge from knowledge that works.

7.3 The Comedy Games

June 2132

This debate was lively, and longlasting, and was most clearly expressed at the close of what came to be known as the Comedy Games—a series of presentations turning on the works of Richard Pryor, Plato and Thelonious Monk.

Tellem's First Tragedy

May 31, 2132

Those rudimentary games were a direct response to Tellem's First Tragedy, which is widely held to be the first exclusion attempted. Kloz Munro hosted Tellem's presentation on a cool spring evening the last weekend in May, and a floral breeze wafted through the open doors and windows of Kloz's Clauses, the second floor of a half-bombed machine-tool factory, in which the first floor had been used for storage, and the loading and unloading of shipments and orders. He lived and worked in the non-bombed half, an open space with no walls and enough room for his records, his drums, his bands, and his friends. Tellem had asked him to dim the room but for a spotlight shining down on an empty music stand. He approached out of the darkness and arranged his presentation papers on it. He started dramatically: "Disprove this." He then went on to elaborate a hypothesis of the slow-motion collapse of the United States as a result of snakebearer social and economic policy. He spoke in the voices of John Erlichman, Milton Friedman, Augusto Pinochet, Oliver North, Donald Trump, "Freeway" Ricky Ross, George HW Bush, Carlos Salinas, Félix Gallardo, William Casey, Bill Clinton, Newt Gingrich, Al Sharpton, Barack Obama, and Alex Jones, presenting material from documents on the New York Central Park Five, the 1968 US Presidential campaign, real-estate investment trusts, integration, desegregation and economic resegregation, the Mexican Drug War, tax shelters and tax avoidance and offshore tax havens, privatization, New Deal and Great Society welfare policy, the 1994 Omnibus Crime Bill, Operation Condor, Vietnam, gerrymandering, both black and white replacement theories, school finance, the Supreme Court, the triangle trade, the Golden Triangle, and heroin, crack, methamphetamine and fentanyl.

The original colonizers of the Western hemisphere attempted to clear the area for exploitation, trying their level best to destroy those who lived there already. They brought slaves from the old world, and built a new world around those slaves. This resulted in a state with two faces: one set against the world it sought to destroy, and the other set against the workers within the new world it was building. They succeeded, in a manner of speaking, and their New World swallowed the old world whole over the next 482 years.

Snakebearer policy had therefore always been genocidal and "racist," but economic pressures that had been building since the end of World War II exploded during and after the Vietnam War, compelling the rulers of the United States, now a world empire, to turn even against their sympathizers, who, in their vicious ignorance demanded greater cruelty. United States policy became increasingly poisonous, the rulers ever more callous and grasping, selling foreign policy and trade agreements for quarterly profits, selling public infrastructure and domestic policy for job opportunities and potential shares of unspecified future revenues, and partnering with criminal organizations at all levels of society, particularly in labor, race relations, and municipal government. Truly, the state had become a union of snakes.

The business of the United States had always been business, but the generalization of the inward-facing brutality and dehumanization that had been reserved for the blacks was extended to all, and this ripped North American society apart such that even everyday commerce was impossibilized. Small businesses closed from rising costs and employees no longer willing to offer anything other than that for which they were paid cold, hard cash; stores shuttered from organized theft, banks hampered and delayed withdrawals, and only the largest enterprises could survive, with state support, and therefore only on terms negotiated with politicians and their organized-crime partners, the latter of whom received ever-increasing money revenues from the destruction, corruption and enslavement of large swathes of the already ruthlessly exploited population. Their money power rose, flourishing in the dark, keeping prices high, and supporting otherwise fraudulent and bankrupt enterprises as money-laundering vehicles in reverse, via secondary markets in shares and derivatives, while capital—investments and products capable of re-entering the economy as inputs to productive enterprise—disintegrated. With perpetual Federal Reserve Board intervention the end of the business cycle became the new focus of capital accumulation: any enterprise capable of generating "growth" during the cycle—legitimate, fraudulent, or criminal—could issue shares and debt, and the more shares in retirement accounts, and the more debt on the books of the widest variety of banks and investment vehicles, the more important the business at the end of the cycle, when the FRB floated free-money loans to primary dealers and thereby systemically important debtors. Instead of clearing the market, the end of the business cycle came to eliminate the competition and reward the most irresponsible or criminal or fraudulent enterprises. The erosion of its economic might was precisely the destruction of the United States and, its world-class enterprises hollowed out, its population languishing in despair, a series of floods, droughts, and speculative bubbles in pseudo currencies and cyberservices ended in financial collapse, mass unemployment, and an altogether chaotic and disorganized civil war of many sides against every other side.

Quite significant to the inductive plausibility of this hypothesis, and perhaps decisive in the event itself, the rulers of this state, relying on their intelligence services and operatives in the media and the academy, still believed that they could manipulate and control their riven populations with scientific lies and calculated distortions, with planted or redacted records and honeypots of misinformation. These strategies only made things worse and, of course, they lost track of their own lies and distortions.

Tellem concluded that, in the course of the privatization of public services, once provided by the state in its popular democratic-republican form, civil society and thus scientific thought itself had also been privatized, either for business-driven agendas or for the personal pleasure and edification of the truth-seeking hobbyist, and that we must therefore assume all records from the last and most important of the olden days to have been falsified in one way or another. Then he asked D-Man to turn on the lights.

The recordkeepers in attendance were not prepared for such a presentation. Most didn't have such deep exposure to the material, and none were prepared for anything like a hypothesis at all. It turned almost immediately into a debate instead of a cooperative game. That was Tellem's challenge, after all.

"What makes you think racism was so important to this?" asked Kloz, the host. He was quite a talented drummer, never lacking for work to buy or trade for musical recordings, recording equipment, and various instruments, which he rented to teachers who rented them to students. "There was a black president, after all." He grew to be a talented player of the game, zeroing in quickly on the structural supports even of unfamiliar frameworks of presentation.

"That's right. And there are other signs, too," Sugarpie added. She was new to the game, but she was a fighter, and quickly joined the confrontation Tellem proposed. "Like the taboo on interracial relationships was gone way before Obama, and blacks had even reclaimed racial epithets like the word 'nigger,' healing the hurt they once caused."

"I don't know about that," Fila spoke up. "Do you know the comedian Chris Rock?" he asked Sugarpie.

"I do, and I know what you're going to say: you want to say that he used 'nigger' to talk bad about poor blacks, and to separate himself from them," Sugarpie retorted.

"And if one man on a stage is doing that, then it's more than just him in the world doing that," said teacher-for-hire Wascal Chase. He wanted to teach physics, but students quit at matrices, so he usually ended up teaching STEM to Water and Power job seekers.

"Yeah, so it was definitely still hurtful," Fila said. "Especially when used like that, sowing division among the group."

"Showing," corrected Tellem.

"You're right," agreed Fila.

"But look, no, it could have been more like motivational speech, like encouraging poor blacks to better themselves," Kloz retorted.

"Exactly," Sugarpie agreed. "Tough love. And that only hurts for a little while."

"What's that they used to say… 'rise and grind'?" chuckled Wascal.

" 'Get money!' " Sugarpie chirped. "That was the name of a 'jam' in 1995, by the Notorious BIG and Lil' Kim, expressing a new freedom and individuality, in the context of new opportunities and aspirations of the so-called black youth."

"OK, well, since you brought up Chris Rock," began George Jefferson, an older man, even older than Tellem, who made his living as a housepainter and visual artist. "What about Richard Pryor?"

"Thank you, GJ," said Sugarpie, pleased that her boyfriend had brought him up. She made textiles, mostly for clothes, and she often used pigments and dyes he had created.

"Who is Richard Pryor?" asked Erron.

"Another comedian, older than Chris Rock," GJ said. "He was the first black entertainer to use 'nigger' routinely in public performances among the whites."

"And that shows that Tellem's so-called racism is overblown," finished Sugarpie.

"When did he do that?" Tellem asked.

"He got big in the 1970s," GJ answered. "He was doing shows before that in the 1960s, but he changed everything up."

"Precisely because there was a cultural and spiritual revival in the 1960s," Sugarpie took the baton. "Everything changed… all the old laws, all the old racist policies of the snakebearers."

Tellem moaned hesitantly and asked, "What about Nixon? What about the war on drugs in the 1980s? What about the explosion in the prison population in the 1990s?"

"What about 'em? We're talking about two different things. You're talking about statistics and institutions, and I'm talking about the way people thought about things," Sugarpie said. "The way they really lived their day-to-day lives, outside of the institutions."

" 'Outside of the institutions'?" Tellem spat. "What does that even mean?"

"They can't be unrelated," Fila said, ignoring Tellem's question for the moment. "The use of a single word by a comedian doesn't really stand up to all Tellem has been talking about."

"It's not just a single comedian," continued Sugarpie, unwilling to concede anything. "It was a whole new generation of artists and entertainers, especially musicians. From Sam Cooke to James Brown to Stevie Wonder to Michael Jackson. The New Breed, Black Is Beautiful, Soul Power… And then hip-hop came out of all that, as you know."

"Of course," Fila said.

"So you know there was a whole new thing happening in the United States at that time. Things were a lot less like Jim Crow and people were a lot more accepting of diversity," she concluded.

"Maybe. I don't know. I don't think so," Fila said. "But why don't you work it up for next weekend?"

She did, and the next weekend Sugarpie played her very first game, with Richard Pryor, at her place, the Flying Shuttle.

That Nigger's Crazy (1974)

June 7, 2132

GJ brought chocolate-chip cookies, chocolate-chip-pecan cookies, chocolate-chip-cherry-pecan cookies, brownies, and hash brownies, a cornucopia of chewy crispy chocolate confections. There were pitchers of fresh mare's milk and goat's milk on ice. He assured everyone that the hash brownies were only very lightly hashed, and he put them by themselves on their own little end table next to the big one, clearly marked. Sugarpie bragged about how they had roasted the pecans and the walnuts, on their own, before putting them into the cookies and brownies. It made a big difference to the taste.

It was not hard to tie the album to the cultural revolution upon which her entire thesis rested, considering that it was recorded at the Soul Train Club in San Francisco's North Beach, and that Pryor had immersed himself in Bay Area politics and culture starting in 1971.

Sugarpie began with the argument that Pryor's use of "nigger" was a sign that the interracial counterculture of the 1960s had achieved such political coherence and ethical power that it could throw caution about such matters as offensive ethnic slurs to the wind, so certain was it of its victory over the old world, so sure was it of its own innocence and purity of heart. She allowed that it was still a counterculture, though, because his audiences clearly delighted not only in Pryor's stories and jokes, but also in being able to take pleasure in Pryor's open use of the word, which was then still taboo.

The questions came thick and fast, within the first several minutes, the first couple of jokes. Sugarpie lifted the needle before "Wino Dealing With Dracula."

"How do we know he's not just freaking out the squares?" Tellem asked, doing his best to use the lingo.

"Ain't no squares in that club," Sugarpie responded with a grin.

GJ laughed and said "Right on, sister."

Fila chuckled and raised his left fist in a black-power salute.

"I'm hip, but most of the audience ain't in the club," jived Wascal.

"Meaning is made on the spot, and that's what's laid down after all is said and done. I say the record-players get the whole experience, and I don't think they can miss it," replied Sugarpie.

"We can't know a man's mind, except by what he says...," Fila began. "But a single man's mind ain't meaning. Meaning is social."

"Agreed," allowed Sugarpie.

"So, there's different ways things can be received. Even if we don't know what went down per se in the event at the given time, we can see the possibilities, and so we know what might have gone down," Fila continued.

"Granted," said Sugarpie.

"Eliminate the extraneous possibilities," Tellem said.

" 'When you have eliminated the impossible, whatever remains, however improbable, must be the truth' ," quoted Kloz.

"That's all square business, but we need to be able to feel the range of possibility deep in our bones. We don't know so much… So, how do we know that Pryor's use of that word, even, or even especially, among the hip, wasn't something more corrupt, like an invitation to a sort of private counterculture, a semi-public ritual in which Pryor absolves his white audience members of historical guilt and shame for the price of a concert ticket?"

"Like the Catholic Church selling indulgences," said GJ.

Fila nodded. "Yeah, that's right."

"That doesn't even need to happen in the club," Wascal added.

"Because the technology, the recording, affords both the pure local experience and other ones," Fila said. "We don't know which happened or if it was both or just one or what."

Sugarpie listened calmly. "I think you're underestimating the power of the change at work here, and the possibility that the new hope overpowered the other possibilities. It would look the same, and we could have the same discussion."

"Or maybe Pryor was just foolish to leave such a gaping ambiguity in his work?" Kloz offered.

"And now you've circled back to my point," Sugarpie noted. "All we've been doing is raising the stakes, putting meat on the bones, seeing the real issues involved in the renewal and social change of the time. Remember, I'm proposing that Pryor's work was *not* ambiguous. Like Fila said, we lack the feeling of the lifeworld of that time, so we don't see right away how he was received the way I propose."

Those gathered realized that she was right—this was, indeed, precisely her point. They had circled back around. Fila still wanted to argue for the range of possibilities, but he didn't, because it didn't speak to Sugarpie's hypothesis. Both could be true. But he felt like he was missing something. Sugarpie dropped the needle back down on "Flying Saucers," and Pryor pulled laughs out of example after example of ongoing racial prejudice and state oppression of the black population of the United States in the 1970s. All the questions that had seemed foreclosed at the end of the first half were reopened.

"The man wouldn't be a comedian doing this show, or maybe even at all, if racism weren't ongoing into the 1970s," Tellem claimed. "What would he be talking about?"

Fila agreed. "Yeah. I know you still think a spirit of renewal is at work here, but you have to allow that the oppression was ongoing," Fila challenged Sugarpie.

"I never said the oppression was over," Sugarpie responded. "I said that the counterculture was confident it would win, and that this new spirit enabled Pryor's comedy and gave it meaning. The battle had been joined, and they were already changing the world, in many ways."

"What about the police brutality?" Kloz asked. "That's state repression, and that's official. That goes to Tellem's…theory."

"Not if the people are busy making a new world," Sugarpie stated.

Fila frowned and twisted his lips in confusion. He closed his eyes.

"I think we have to look at the possibility Fila raised," Wascal said. "That would betray your new hope."

"I don't see how," Sugarpie responded. "We don't have a way to compare the weight of the new spirit against any corruption afforded by the recording medium, but we do have a whole lot of changes in the world, and many more blacks flourishing and creating in the decades after the 1960s."

"You want to look at data here but not there," said Tellem. "You want to tally up salaries? Count the heads of business leaders and elected officials?"

Fila said "Yeah," though his eyes were still closed.

"Why not?" asked Sugarpie. "You count prisoners."

"I proposed that the state expanded its repression beyond the blacks, but continued it without improving their position. Blacks were no longer singled out in the law, but repression…repression became colorblind, and that didn't mean that blacks escaped, but that more people were caught in circumstances formerly reserved to the blacks," Tellem responded.

"Slavery and segregation are fundamentally economic relationships," Fila added, opening his eyes.

"Exactly," said Tellem.

"ok, but what about this mass-market sale of indulgences?" Wascal rejoined. "The fact that we can't weigh the pure hearts of the hip against the corrupt practices enabled by anonymous mass distribution isn't an answer, because you have to admit that it's possible that the one outweighed the other."

"You know what I am going to say, right?" asked Sugarpie.

"That Pryor's work is still an embodied performance of the new spirit, and that this is all that you have claimed?" asked Wascal.

"Yes," Sugarpie said.

"ok, but doesn't it mean something if that spirit is just hemmed in on all sides?" Wascal continued.

"That's where I have to point to the evidence of growing black representation in the arts and in business and government," Sugarpie said.

"But again, we know that the laws changed," Wascal continued. "Blacks could get elected and get better jobs. But we also know what Tellem told us last week, that the repression hitting the majority both of the black population and the broader population was essentially the same or worse, even though it was colorblind."

"I don't see how that changes anything," Sugarpie responded.

"Maybe the representation you're talking about is also like an indulgence," Wascal replied. "They called it tokenism."

"Maybe with the politicians and business people, but not with the artists. Something clearly broke loose in the 1960s," Sugarpie argued. "And it continued into the twenty-first century."

"You relied on context to judge the new spirit in Pryor's work," said Wascal. "Even though you now admit that the new spirit can be outweighed by its context. You have to admit that later developments must be subject to the same possibility: corruption in the medium allowing them to be outweighed by bad context, hemmed in by their broader reception."

"Oh!" Fila exclaimed. "Yeah! That's right. You're begging the question. You assume context to show that Pryor's 'nigger's are spirited and not corrupt or foolish, but then you reject context showing that they might be corrupt or foolish, because Pryor's 'nigger's are spirited."

"That's what I've been saying the whole time," Tellem said.

"I know. You're right. I was just trying to think of the name of it. It's a circular argument. It's slippery too, though, because there was such a big social change, and things did look so different," Fila said.

"But now," Fila continued, turning toward Sugarpie, "it seems like you cannot possibly adequately address the question of the corruption afforded by the medium—tokenism and the sale of indulgences—because you have to show the spirit's effects beyond these individual artifacts you've been using. You mentioned that we lack the feel of the lifeworld of that time. You have to show that spirit creating significant supportive context, and you just can't do that with what we have. We can reconstruct some sort of mosaic, but we can't tell how important the pieces are in relation to each other."

"Well, listen," Sugarpie began. "I don't know why I have to do that. First of all, I still think the body of work created after the civil rights movement stands as evidence of something liberatory, even if I might not be able to prove it, just with the records themselves."

This seemed like the beginning of a humble concession of defeat, couched in defensive language.

"And second of all," she continued, "artists are not responsible for the reception of their work."

Kloz's Clauses erupted into a cacophony of shouts, denunciations, jeers, curses, and abuse.

"Oh, but no."

"After all that spirit jive, too?"

"Now she comes with this?"

"I know she didn't."

"Oh, yes, she did."

"Niggers still ain't got no sense."

Sugarpie has never admitted that this was a copout. She attempted to withdraw it and reground her position in the individual artist's practice of comedy.

"It's all about the work," she yelled, but they shouted her down. GJ tried to quiet the room, and they shouted him down too.

Kloz was laughing with Wascal and Tellem was amirth with chuckles, so Fila figured he had to be the one to do something in the way of moderation. He gestured to Sugarpie that he would be speaking next, then he stood, and the jeering died down a little bit.

"I'm game! Let's talk about Pryor's work more closely, then," he began, as though nothing had happened. "It's mostly stories. He uses 'nigger' in vernacular stories about the blacks, just like they did in their everyday lives. That tells us that it's not the word, but it's the stories that are important. And the stories are important, notable at all, because he is telling the so-called white folks, who haven't heard them before."

"Nice," said Kloz. There was broad assent. Sugarpie agreed as well, so Fila continued.

"But they're funny like all humor, because of surprises and violated expectations. Like a crazy answer to a normal question. Or putting the emphasis on the wrong word. What do you think?" Fila asked Sugarpie.

She had remained seated by the record player. "I agree. Comedy is mostly surprise surprise, or shock, or subverted expectations. That's no crime or corruption, though." She was feeling a bit defensive.

"OK, but it has to be funny, right?" Fila asked.

"Yes, it does, and he was. That's the only way he became important. Well, that and the social changes preceding his own transformation, which include the spiritual renewal and the broadcast and communications technologies, which had been around, but they were dominated by the old order."

"Are you about to go back on your context trip?" asked Kloz.

"No, I'm just saying… maybe his work was countercultural, fighting against a bad context, like Wascal said, and maybe that context overwhelmed it. We don't know," she finally admitted. "But that whole counterculture had an aspirational aspect to it, and that demanded that artists sometimes perform aspirationally."

"Encouraging and inspiring the audience," GJ said.

"Exactly," Sugarpie said.

"What about Lenny Bruce? He was a white comedian using the word 'nigger' a decade before," asked D-Man.

"That was before the laws changed," Sugarpie argued.

"And Bruce didn't have Pryor's experience and stories," said Fila.

"I think you might be on to something with this aspiration," Wascal said. "Social change has a cost, and somebody has to pay. If there was a new spirit, its bearers had to make sacrifices, even to find each other. But how can you establish trust? Somebody has to step up and step out."

"Even losing a war somebody has to wave the white flag," said Fila.

"And trust they won't get killed," said Tellem.

"The warriors share values, like chivalry and honor," Fila noted.

Wascal continued. "So it might even look like selling indulgences, but it could be much more complicated. On one level Pryor is an individual seeking acceptance for his outrageous conflicted self. On another level he's offering himself as a focus of the social conlicts. It's not insincere, because he himself is conflicted and hurt, and so he's a good example. On the third level, he is trusting the audience to laugh with him, thereby to share and bear the past with him. Maybe only the hippest can go all the way, and the rest would end up having bought an indulgence. But somebody has to do it. And it only works if it's funny."

"Very nice," Sugarpie nodded approval, pleased that someone was building on any part of her work so far.

"I want to agree with you, in a way, too," Fila added. "On shared context. You had wanted to say that Pryor's work embodied a context—a spirit of rejuvenation. But I want to go the other way… Twentieth-century Americans had shared assumptions about family dynamics. He said, nope. Not mine. They had shared expectations about how men and women should get along, and he said, nope, not over here, not for a long time."

"OK, but what's backward, what's reversed?" Sugarpie asked.

"He was airing a bunch of dirty laundry," Fila said. "His stories showed how people couldn't live those assumptions and aspirations— shared values—because of social conflicts like racism."

"You're saying he was revealing the shared values by showing how they were violated," added Kloz.

"Because dirty laundry is still laundry, and everybody has some idea about how dirty it can get," added GJ.

"Right," Fila continued. "So instead of arguing that Pryor's work represents this or that, which you can't really prove, you can argue that it reveals that this or that must be true."

"Or false," added Tellem.

"I don't see why not," Fila said. "But the whole thing is, Pryor is trying to put twentieth-century American society back together again, in a way, by showing the similarities in the differences. The more shocking the difference, the bigger the laugh, and the clearer the basis of judgment: the shared values."

"And how do you know those shared values are different from the ones of the spirit of renewal?" Sugarpie asked, trying to pin down the distinction.

"They are different. The values have to be shared for the comedy to exist, for the jokes to work. Not the other way around, that the comedy shows some values to exist. The values I'm talking about are therefore prior to any spirit of renewal, and they are the basis of any spirit of renewal, if it existed. I think it's just all the old humanist stuff, the rights of man, *liberté, égalité, fraternité*," Fila answered. "Pryor is taking black and white, the expected and unexpected, and, by the exposure of egregious, violent, shocking difference, revealing what the people have in common. He's reminding everybody that they are a unity already, anyway."

"Yeah, remembering the unity of a whole. Remembering literally means to re-member, to put something back together, that had been dis-membered," Wascal said.

"You said it," Fila agreed. Folks had started to pack up.

"Listen," Tweety Bird Andrews stood and yawned. A poet and electrician, Tweety was something of a social butterfly, at ease anywhere, impressive everywhere, and women were often eager for his attention. So they watched when he moved, and everyone listened when he spoke. "Y'all know Richard Pryor changed his mind about 'nigger', right?"

"What do you mean?" asked Sugarpie, carefully lifting the album off the turntable.

"Yeah, in *Live on the Sunset Strip* in 1982. That was his first show after setting himself on fire smoking cocaine, and taking a trip to Africa. He had a change of heart about the way it was being received."

"Is that right?" asked Tellem.

"It is," continued Tweety.

"Why didn't you say something earlier?" asked Fila.

"I wanted to see what you niggers came up with," he grinned. That was good for a few laughs.

"Wordplay is great," Kloz said, standing and stretching. "But part of why we got caught in that loop earlier was because we were dealing with words trying to make meaning of words."

"Good point," said Fila. "Trying to figure out if these words are good or bad using other words from elsewhere that might also be good or bad."

"Let's talk about comedy in a different key," Kloz proposed. "No words. Next week I want to play you all some Thelonious Monk, a piano player from around the same time."

"Out of sight," said Fila.

"Righteous," said Wascal.

"Far out," agreed Sugarpie.

"I'm not hip," said Tellem, who stood to show off his injured leg, clack his cane, and crack a smile. "But I will be."

Thelonious Monk, "Body and Soul," *Monk's Dream* (1963)

June 14, 2132

The aroma of fresh-baked bread filled Kloz's Clauses, as he had a table full of French-style baguettes sliced into sections for the taking. He had cut thin slices from a whole leg of dried and cured North Carolina ham, which he displayed prominently on the table, and he had laid out an assortment of cheeses—a Munster from Connecticut, a wheel of soft triple cream from Upstate New York, mozzarella from Maine, aged cheddar from Vermont. There were jars of blackberry and raspberry preserves, and several wines—Virginia Rieslings, some Pennsylvania Pinots, and a dry sparkling blueberry wine from New Hampshire.

Kloz opened his game with no words, as promised. He simply put the record on and played it. When the song was over, he sat silently.

"ok…," began Wascal, hesitant.

"What the hell was that?" asked Sugarpie.

Kloz passed her the album cover. " 'Body and Soul,' recorded in March 1963. That's during the civil rights movement, but before the laws were changed," she said.

"What are we supposed to think? I thought you were going to say something about comedy?" Carnation asked. Carnation Adams was Pastor Snap Arnold's sister Kullers's daughter-in-law, from her husband Presto Adams's first marriage to a woman named Skysong, *née* Street. Presto and Skysong also had a son, Erron, Carnation's brother. She was the youngest recordkeeper then, at 18, but she was sharp. She and Fila had been courting for a few weeks.

"I can't follow the melody?" asked Wascal.

"And it's the opposite of funny," Fila offered. "It sounds like somebody being disappointed."

"I agree. It's not much of a song at all, but if it is, it's mournful," suggested Tellem. "But there's something weird about it. Like he can't figure out exactly how he's supposed to feel."

"But the bass line seems consistently sad," said GJ.

Kloz nodded and smiled. He took the cover from Sugarpie and resleeved *Monk's Dream*, and then he put on Coleman Hawkins's *Body & Soul*, and dropped the needle into the groove of the title track.

"Well, that's not the same song at all," sighed Tellem. Kloz passed him the album cover.

"Let's see… It's supposed to be the same song, but this one is from 1939," Tellem announced.

"I guess I like it," said D-Man. "It sounds less sad."

"The feelings are still confused, I think," said Carnation.

"I think it's still mournful," said Fila. "But I can't really tell they're the same song. And it's certainly not funny."

Tellem returned the cover, and Kloz put on the third album, replacing Coleman Hawkins's *Body & Soul* with Billie Holiday's *Body and Soul.* The guitar strummed in.

Sugarpie was weeping before the second verse. GJ sniffed.

"Now that's a song," said Tellem.

"Ooh, wee, now she's singing something," said Fila, surreptitiously wiping a tear from his nose. "Who is that?"

Kloz handed him the cover. "Billie Holiday, 1957," Fila reported.

"That's beautiful," agreed Carnation, swaying in her seat.

"It's sentimental," said Wascal, voice cracking. He cleared his throat. "Is that the same thing as sad?"

Kloz shrugged suggestively, lifting his eyebrows, maintaining his wordlessness.

"Good question," Sugarpie said. "I think it sort of is. But sentimental can't be only sad. It needs something else. Fila said 'disappointed' earlier…"

"You can't be disappointed unless you were hopeful," said D-Man.

"So to be touching, the song needs to be a mix," GJ said. "And that can be confusing, like Tellem said."

"OK, but what does any of this have to do with comedy?" asked Sugarpie, eager to get to wherever Kloz was trying to go.

"Since he's not saying anything," Fila began, giving Kloz a sly eye, "let's remember what he said. He said he wanted to do this because words got us turned around before, and we couldn't tell cause from effect or subject from object. We couldn't tell whether Pryor was embodying or resisting or representing or corrupting. We got confused. I think Kloz is trying to say something about communicating contradictory things."

"Yeah, but we're all still confused," Wascal chuckled.

"Not about this song," Carnation said. "This song is absolutely clear and beautiful and sad."

"It's also the only version of the song with words," D-Man noted, to murmurs of appreciation from those gathered.

Kloz rose dramatically to retrieve the Holiday album cover, and he put her album away. He pulled out another, much smaller record, and presented it to everyone: Louis Armstrong and His Sebastian New Cotton Club Orchestra. He put it on.

Everyone was horrified.

"This is nothing like that woman, what's her name, singing this song," said Wascal.

"Billie Holiday," said Fila.

"He ain't right," said Sugarpie.

"He's making a mockery of it!" said Carnation.

"He's a vandal," said D-Man.

"Why did you play that mess after what's her name?" said Tellem.

"Billie Holiday," said Sugarpie.

"When is this?" Wascal asked.

Kloz passed him the album cover.

"Oh, wow. This is from 1930," Wascal said. "That's the earliest one we've heard."

"Older ain't necessarily better," said Carnation.

Kloz stood and finally spoke. "That's not only the oldest we've heard, but that's the first recorded version ever. And it looks like everybody hates it."

No one enjoyed hearing that fact. "I feel like you might be playing *us*," said Tellem. "Distorting the record." Fila grunted and folks started grumbling a little.

"I admit it. I did distort the record," Kloz said. "But only by playing them out of order."

"I still can't quite see what this musical exploration has to do with the last game," said D-Man. "Not yet, anyway."

"It's about context, and what it's made out of," Kloz continued. "It was obvious that Pryor was engaged in some sort of social struggle, so the context was society. He is a man struggling against society. He is a subject working on that object. But that's not enough to be able to decide anything about his work from the record of his work. In fact, it's not even really true, because he comes out of a part of that society, and he's been affected by it, and both subject and object are conflicted. He's all messed up and so is society, in the same way. There's a sort of undecidable, indeterminate oscillation of subject and object, what Fila was just talking about. And that's why a bunch of intellectuals genuinely got caught in a circular argument last Saturday."

"So what's the context here, with music?" asked Tellem.

"Exactly," answered Kloz. "And how could playing it out of order cause such a problem? We didn't know how to hear the two instrumental versions, 24 years apart. Billie's vocal version, in between those two, is so beautiful it can make you cry. That's when we figured out what the song was about," Kloz said. "But that's not really what the song is about at all. That was an illusion, like an optical illusion, except in history."

"The words took over," nodded Sugarpie.

"A lexical illusion," Fila added.

"But it's not just the words, because the same words made everybody mad when Armstrong sang them," Carnation said.

"So what makes the difference?" Wascal concluded the thought.

"The structure of feeling," Kloz answered. "Music is so flexible that you can make the same song sound and feel many different ways, obviously. It's flexible because it's abstract. Billie's words nailed it down, removed the ambiguity, and it actually froze our hearts in a particular posture. Armstrong's original somehow became offensive to our frozen hearts."

"I wonder what would have happened if Armstrong wasn't singing," asked Fila.

"Good question," said Sugarpie.

"Probably the same confusion as with the other instrumental versions," Kloz said. "There's something similar going on here to what was going on in Pryor's work," he continued. "The mixture of the hope and the disappointment, the mourning and the morning. This musical idiom in particular is known for exactly that. But for us, without words, all we could do was identify the most basic emotions like sad and arguably hopeful, but we couldn't draw anything out of the conflict between them, not like Fila identified the shared context, the assumptions and values lurking in the background of Pryor's work in the 1970s."

"The clash was not fruitful," offered Fila.

"Not yet," granted Kloz. "With Pryor, he was clearly the subject, and society, his object, was also the context. With music, it's not clear what the subject and object even are, let alone any shared context. But because I know, I'll tell you that modern music, from the turn of the nineteenth century on, with Beethoven, chose subjectivity itself as the object, so the artifacts are a record of the self-development of the creative subject."

"In music, you mean?" asked Fila.

"Yes, of course," agreed Kloz.

"If it's all subjective, then who's to know what's being communicated?" asked Tellem.

"Subjective doesn't mean solipsistic," Kloz answered. "There is a shared context, and it is still social, but it's not like Pryor's work. Subjects and objects normally make history in time, but music just puts sound into time. You need some sort of way into it."

"Like what?"

"Some sort of cultural key that lets you understand what the musicians are doing. The way they're evolving the structures of feeling, changing how they're built, new feelings they're trying to express, what they have to say about the old ways and old feelings, and on and on like that," Kloz said.

"What, you can't mean that we need to learn how to put it together?" asked Fila. "We need to become musicians?"

"No, we just need the contextual knowledge. Familiarity, basically. In this case, how to listen to it. But that's lived culture, and so you can't assume that you know how to listen to it, even if it seems obvious. Like we can't say that Billie's version is the right one or the best one, just because it comes through best," Kloz said. "It's the same kind of knowledge Sugarpie was trying to conjure out of Pryor's 'nigger's, imputing knowledge to the audience. But that's a logical fallacy. Here our feelings hardened, and we were prejudiced against other expressions."

"An emotional fallacy," chuckled Wascal.

"Exactly. And the thing about Louis Armstrong's version is that even in the 1930s, musicians like him were sort of poking fun at the material they had to work with, taking it tongue in cheek. He sings the lyrics however he wants, whimsically, like to say they don't really matter, and they're sort of silly, aren't they? Hawkins sounds like he's making fun of the song, too, but it's more sophisticated, because he's doing it with no words. He has to do it with the melody, making it sound self-serious and just barely not ridiculous. Holiday, as we know, sings the hell out of the song, pouring her own body and soul into it. It's not funny, and it's not ironic—it's just soulful. Monk, finally, just shatters the song, and plays like a child with the pieces, now almost unrecognizable, but in a musical structure that he helped to invent, and that was by then familiar to listeners, and capable of conveying subtle shades of feeling. Holiday is the odd one out here, not Armstrong, Monk, or Hawkins."

Carnation nodded her reluctant assent.

"And that's my joke on you," Kloz said. "Because modern music is the record of the subject reflecting on its own development, its own sense depends on that chronology. I tricked everybody by changing the order."

"OK, but you're almost making it sound like music should be totally opaque without familiarity with the structures," GJ said. "So how were we able to understand any of the emotions in the instrumental versions?"

"I don't know how to explain that," Kloz admitted, "except to say that maybe there's something about certain harmonies having a certain effect on the brain and therefore the mind—maybe musical structures correspond quite physically to structures of feeling. Or maybe it's just cultural knowledge lingering, surviving, even after all this…"

"And how could we ever decide that?" asked Sugarpie.

"Very, very carefully," yawned Fila, who stood and stretched.

"We have a lot of memory going on here," Wascal said, handing Kloz back the Armstrong 45 cover. "We have Pryor recalling unity in shared values honored in the breach and we have a mysterious musical memory, which could be either biological or cultural."

"Well put," said Carnation.

"I want to see if I can tie all this together," Wascal said. "Music and memory, I mean. Plato has some good stuff on this, so I'd like to do something next week."

"Let's do it," said Fila. "Next week at Wascal's Wadius, everybody! Don't forget!"

Anamnesis, *Meno* & *Somnium Scipionis*

June 21, 2132

Wascal stood in a white toga behind a table in front of the bay window on the first floor of his record store, with the curtains drawn, so that the room was only electricly lumined. Kloz had a drum kit set up just inside the large parlor, next to the refreshments, which were entirely vegetarian. Wascal had platters of celery, snap peas, carrots, pitas, and hummus; tahini, chili sauces, olives, and multiple pickles, from cucumbers and radishes to red onions and cauliflower. There were solid blocks of ice for water (that he distilled himself with an ingenious solar-powered system of pipes and bottles), juices fruit and vegetable, and ciders hard and soft.

He held up a rectangular wood frame, perhaps $2' \times 10''$, into which was pinned a rectangle of rough jute burlap, which was dyed black. The burlap fabric flopped out past the edges of the frame, because it was only held to the frame in the corners. One could see each thread of the quite coarse cloth's warp and woof. He laid the frame on the table, and then he painted a bright, glittery white stick figure on it. The contrast was sufficient to cause the figure to shimmer against its ground.

"Thanks GJ, Sugarpie, for the materials," he said, nodding in their direction. "I want to start with this picture," he said, holding it up. "Let's say this is somebody listening to music."

"If you say so," said Carnation, chuckling at Wascal's crude drawing.

"Where's the boom box?"

"Can we get a drum at least?"

Wascal grinned and motioned toward the back of the room. "Kloz? You heard." Kloz began a slow and steady kick on the bass drum.

He went on. "Before the war of Actium in 32 BCE brought an end to the Roman Republic, there was a general named Publius Cornelius Scipio, probably the noblest noble in human history. That's the man who defeated Hannibal at Carthage in 202 BCE, and he became known as Scipio Africanus."

He had the group's attention then, and they were eager for him to rise to the challenge he appeared to be setting himself.

"The people loved this man: both his soldiers and the plebians. He was a land reformer, and made sure that his soldiers received some upon retirement. We don't know what the proletarians thought, but they probably followed the plebians. He could have declared himself emperor after that victory over Hannibal, and a couple of other times after that. As you can imagine, the other aristocrats were jealous. Cato hated his guts." Wascal touched the white paint of his skeletal auditor to see if it was dry. It was not.

"But he was a real republican. He didn't want to be a dictator. He stayed a general, opened embassies, and kept winning battles. His enemies tried to bribe him to settle a battle, so that they could later impeach his victory as the fruit of corruption. They even tried to frame him for misappropriation of war plunder. I said misappropriation of war plunder. Cato brought bribery charges against him on the anniversary of his defeat of Hannibal, and Scipio wiped the floor with him in the Senate, and then led a mass march to church," Wascal continued. "The temple of Jupiter, anyway."

"Bless his heart," said Carnation.

Wascal gestured Kloz, who increased the tempo.

"But do you see what I'm saying? Somehow, this man sidestepped his enemies' every trick, every trap, every plot to destroy him and his reputation. With unerring accuracy, repeatedly, for years. How?"

"Good luck?" chuckled Tellem.

"God's favor," offered Fila.

"*Fortuna*!" yelled D-Man.

"The man was actually noble," Wascal went on. "He loved the ladies, and so one time, his enemies tried to trick him into stirring up war again in a nearly pacified Carthaginian Iberia—Spain—by delivering him a beautiful woman they had captured in battle. They expected that he would use her as plundered war booty, but he didn't. He investigated and found out that she was engaged to one of the potential belligerents, and he returned her to her fiancé, unransomed and unmolested." Some of those gathered muttered appreciation.

"That was such rare behavior that artists painted the event for centuries after his death. The man was a legend of intellect and virtue, *in his own time*: a true gentleman and scholar. A Hellenophile, he spoke, read, and wrote Greek. He was a legendary general. He was obviously a great orator. He set fashion trends. Folks said he had second sight—premonitions in dreams and visions—and even his enemies believed that he communicated directly with the gods. He probably believed it, too." Wascal held up his hand for Kloz to cease drumming.

Wascal paced ponderously, as though gathering his thoughts. He then gestured for Kloz to begin the beat again, original tempo, slowly, steadily, like an advancing Roman phalanx.

"So how does a man end up so different from those around him?" Wascal asked, checking whether his drawing was dry. "What do you think, Fila?"

"Er, I don't know. I guess he just somehow had a different temperament," Fila answered.

"He may have had better teachers," offered D-Man.

"All the nobles had the same teachers, more or less," Wascal said. "And how was he different, anyway?"

"He was just a better man," said Carnation.

"But what do you mean by 'better'?" Wascal asked.

"He wasn't a jealous-hearted snake in the grass, for one," she answered.

"Seems obvious he was smarter," said Tellem.

"He was decent," Vinilla offered.

"So he had a more developed moral sense?" asked Wascal.

"That's a good way to put it," said Carnation.

"What's a moral sense?" asked Wascal. "I mean, what does a moral sense sense?"

"Just basic morality. Justice, goodness," Carnation answered.

"So, something like virtue," Wascal asked.

"That's right," she answered.

"Is there one virtue or are there many?"

"Hmm… there are many virtues," Carnation answered.

"What is 'virtue', then?" Wascal asked.

" 'Virtue' is being virtuous, doing virtuous things," Carnation said.

"So doing virtue makes one virtuous."

"Obviously."

"So, how do you know any of those things, the many virtues, are virtuous?"

"Well, because… oh, I see," Carnation said. "Because they're virtuous."

"Right. You can't identify the thing that unites the virtues—virtue itself seems to slip away every time. We just recreated part of *Meno*, one of Plato's Socratic dialogues. Socrates showed Meno that virtue can't be taught, because if it could, no wise man would ever have a foolish child, and more people would be virtuous. After going through the whole thing, Socrates concludes that virtue is simply the way God's gifts to the virtuous appear. Virtue is an instinct granted the eternal soul before birth, and virtuous action is the way it looks when that soul re-members its divine gifts. As for Tellem's remark about intelligence, Plato has Socrates say 'Nor is the instinct accompanied by reason, unless there may be supposed to be among statesmen any one who is also the educator of statesmen.' So, not even Scipio could explain his *fortuna*, as D-Man put it.

"Now, appropriately, near the end of the Roman Republic, it's greatest thinkers were struck with melancholy. They knew the age of such heroes was coming to an end. They knew themselves to be decadent. They had only to look in the mirror. One of those thinkers was Marcus Tullius Cicero, a philosopher and historian. He wrote a story lamenting the loss of such men, but recalling their immortality to his contemporaries.

"In that story, Scipio Aemilianus, the grandson of Scipio Africanus, is on the verge of defeating Carthage once and for all, finishing the job his grandfather started. Africanus was not his grandfather by blood, but by adoption. Anyway, Aemilianus has a dream in which his grandfather visits him and takes his soul on a tour of the galaxy, to show him how the revolutions of the sun, i.e., the measure of human historical reckonings, can hardly even be compared to the revolutions of the galaxy, let alone the scales that reckon eternity. It's a shockingly visual demonstration, and probably one of the first illustrations of the lesson that we have to live our lives in accord with eternity, the only measure appropriate to the eternal immortal soul.

"Africanus also shows his grandson that the universe is arranged into concentric spheres of heavenly bodies, the outermost being the realm of the gods. Then the stars, and then Saturn, Jupiter, Mars, Sun, Venus, Mercury, Moon, and finally Earth, the lowest. They make sounds as they revolve in their unequal intervals, and that's the harmony of the spheres, the *musica universalis*." Kloz drummed several flourishes, filling more of the space between the steady beats of the bass drum.

"I want some of what they were on, OK?" said GJ in a stage whisper, while ribbing Tweety Bird.

"I don't think you could handle it," replied Tweety, in mock confidence.

"So we live in an actual octave, according to Cicero. Most people are deaf to the music of the universe because it's so loud, but Cicero's Africanus is saying that by turning our attention to our eternal souls, we can tune ourselves to these cosmic frequencies."

Wascal paused and Kloz played a bit, rolling some rhythms into one another.

"Cicero wrote this story, and this whole book, *De Re Publica*, from within the Platonic tradition, and no one who read the story then doubted that it was a version of Plato's own Myth of Er, in the *Republic*, where a man killed in battle visits the underworld, only to be resurrected, and to tell of all he found there. Plato used Er to illustrate Socrates's idea of *anamnesis*, an anti-amnesia, un-forgetting, re-membering. The idea is basically that true knowledge is only ever recalled from the time before the soul chose whatever life it is in at the moment."

"Oh, so all this depends on reincarnation, then?" asked Fila.

"Socrates's anamnesis does, but not Cicero's cosmic tuning," answered Wascal. "That just depends on the immortality of the eternal soul. To the Greeks, reincarnation was just a corollary of the immortality of the eternal soul, like an implication."

"You're going to have to explain that," said D-Man.

"They thought about it like this: if the soul is immortal and eternal, what does it do after death? It didn't make sense to them that it would never enter life again, and just sort of hang out doing nothing in the universe. That would be somehow wasteful of cosmic soul stuff, and it would also lead to the afterlife being overcrowded. But I think you can tell that this is just some random cultural stuff. We don't need reincarnation. The important thing is immortality and eternity."

Fila and D-Man accepted this, for the moment, but Tellem did not.

"OK, let's say we don't need reincarnation to make Plato's Socrates's anamnesis work. But what kind of knowledge is he talking about?" Tellem asked.

"Right! Are these folks supposed to know things like the outcomes of sporting events?" asked D-Man.

"Or if it's going to rain on your birthday party," said Carnation. This line of questioning was important to those gathered at Wascal's.

"Good question," Wascal noted. "That came up in *Meno*, too. Plato meant formal knowledge—not data and information, contingent facts—but ideas, methods, and relationships. The moral sense, virtue, for instance, but even geometry. He calls the one knowledge and the other correct opinion. Data is correct opinion. Virtue is not exactly knowledge, as we have seen, but it is more like wisdom, a gift of the gods."

"So what is the knowledge recalled, then?" Tellem asked again.

"In *Meno*, Socrates takes an uneducated slave boy through the process of recreating the Pythagorean theorem, just by asking him questions," Wascal answered. "Socrates delivers no knowledge, but his questions check illogic. Socrates concludes that the boy must have known it already, and since he was never taught them, he must have learned them in a past life, because the soul is eternal."

"Reincarnation again," sighed Fila.

"That's where he takes it, yes," agreed Wascal. "The trauma of birth and the fact that souls bound for life have to take a drink from the river Lethe explains the amnesia. The questions guide the an-amnesia, according to Plato."

"What a story," GJ noted.

"But really, though," Wascal went on. "That's just cultural stuff. We don't need to agree that every immortal soul drinks of oblivion before rebirth to agree with the shape of what he's saying: sometimes knowledge seems to leap to mind without our having 'learned' anything at all. There is no effort, but the knowledge just appears and slides into place."

Wascal gestured to Kloz, and his drumming contracted back to the martial thump of the bass drum. "With music there is time, i.e., rhythm, the foundation of the musical universe." Wascal held up the fabric with the now-dry stick figure. "We all agree that this fabric has a rhythm? The warp and the woof are pretty regular."

Everyone agreed.

"I like this fabric because it's so coarse and rough that you can see the rhythm…" Wascal held the frame up, presenting the figure to the gathering, and then he began pulling at a clump of woof threads on their left-hand side, which immediately distorted the figure's head, giving it something of a squinting expression. "Rhythm changes are immediately perceived, and that perception immediately grants you the knowledge that something new is coming." Kloz had complicated the rhythm as Wascal pulled the threads.

"Speaking of second sight, rhythm changes can tell us what's coming, and sometimes we know the shape of the new thing, too." Wascal tugged at several woof threads from the other side, a little lower, so that the figure shrugged a shoulder, and Kloz moved different parts of the rhythm to different pieces of the drum kit.

"It is important to clearly separate the moments of cognition and recognition, because they are not the same." He pulled woof from the first side to pull the torso away from the shrugged shoulder. "That way we can see that the patterns according to which expectancy is evoked and either satisfied or frustrated can then become a new basis for communication." Wascal threw the figure's hip in the same direction as the shoulder. "But all this is lateral, linear. We've only been working in one dimension." Wascal pulled warp threads at the top of the frame along the figure's left side, lifting both its arm and bending its leg, and Kloz began to move a piece of the rhythm away from the rest, so that there were suddenly two rhythms. "Harmony has rhythm, too, and, likewise, the theory of harmonic tension and release relies on expectations that can be heightened, frustrated, satisfied, etc." Wascal pulled warp threads down on the figure's right side, and it looked like it would break itself dancing. "These are all modalities with which the artist can play to create new structures of feeling.

"I want to suggest to you that this is not only a man listening to music, but for Socrates, Plato, the Scipiones, Cicero, and many more for many years after them, it is also the eternal immortal soul astride, amid, aflight, amongst, the cosmos. The harmony of the spheres is not a metaphor, but the actual mechanism of anamnesis." Wascal painted another stick figure, standing still, to the right of the first, already dancing.

"Recollection, re-membrance, takes place in a context, some sort of fabric, like this coarse weave, or a rhythm, or some web of concrete social relationships… You can see it right here. The first figure has been informed of the change in his universe, and it has directly affected his posture. He knows that something different is happening. It's literally in his body, which is now distorted. He knows what his body used to be. That means he can communicate the change to his companion." Wascal held up the frame, and methodically reversed each of the woof pulls that had distended the first body, thereby transmitting their inverse to the companion figure. Tweety Bird whistled approval and somebody clapped.

"Music communicates a structure of feeling by modifying it," Wascal said. "Recollection itself—knowledge of how the fabric used to be—is the instrument that music plays in the mind of the listener. Music, as heard, is literally memory play: the skillful manipulation of the anamnetic capacity.

"The ridges, the knots, the snags and pulls in the web—this is how the soul reads itself, re-members itself, out of the texture of the fabric of the past, of which it was already the weaver anyway. And so, like Kloz taught us last week, modern music rediscovered its own ancient vocation: to mediate the relation of creative subjectivity to itself."

Kloz crashed a cymbal, ending the music, and the two received more than a little applause. Wascal took an ironically noble bow, and the strap on his toga came aloose, and he fumbled to pull it back up—he was naked underneath except for his boxer shorts—and so the applause turned to goodhearted but embarrassed laughter, which quickly subsided.

"I love everything you're doing here," began Tellem. "But I have a question about the communication. The pulls on the up-down threads were *not* communicated across the fabric. They didn't even touch the new figure."

"You're right. I guess that's probably something that has to be communicated some other way—it can't be read directly out of the web," Wascal answered. "Not this one, anyway. But because the figures are vertical, most of the important stuff about the alignment of the parts of the bodies can be communicated via the woof."

"So some of the information can be lost," Sugarpie said, sadly.

"Absolutely," answered Wascal. "As we know."

"I tried to stay silent as long as I could last week," Kloz added, "but because I played the music out of order, I had to reorder it chronologically. I could only do that, decisively, with words."

"A whole *dimension* of the information can be lost," Fila specified.

"That's bad enough," started Tellem. "But then we have to fall back on the lexical anyway."

"Well, we're not telepathic, either, but we can still communicate a whole lot before we start talking," noted D-Man.

"Yeah, it's not like the music is saying nothing just because it's not saying everything," Tweety Bird agreed. "But Wascal, what is that dimension? What is that one, the up-down axis, the… er…"

"Warp," said Sugarpie.

"Yes, the warp. What does that represent here?" Tweety Bird finished.

"I think it's harmonies in music," Wascal answered. "Because you can interpret that 'vertical' information with a different voicing, even if you have a written harmony. And you can make a whole different harmonization anyway. And it's similar for anamnesis: there's information that may not fit the idiosyncratic events of particular reincarnations of the eternal immortal soul. Like, individual lives won't have the exact same shape, so 'vertical' information won't always apply."

"Literally miss me with your precise arm positions," joked Carnation.

"Or unnecessary cultural baggage," said Wascal.

"ok, but isn't it obvious that we won't be able to reverse engineer all the wrinkles and distortions for everything we want to know?" Tellem asked. "Why shouldn't we just accept, for instance, that Billie Holiday is the one who speaks to us, and build from there? We might find firmer ground to stand on doing it that way, and it might make it easier for us to build bridges to the others."

Fila answered Tellem. "But you *know* Billie is not firm ground. You're just arbitrarily choosing a position out of an unreasoned prejudice. Why not just accept the actual problem you have, which is making sense of the range of possibilities?"

"God has blessed us to discover something so beautiful, so useful, so real to us, here, today, across such a dark and dismal abyss, and you're ready to throw it away and call it prejudice?" Tellem responded. "If that's what it is, then I just might be alright with that, and I doubt I'd be alone."

"Well," Carnation said, looking at Fila.

"It's better to have something that you can work with, something you can build on, than a whole bunch of questions you can't ever hope to answer," Tellem concluded.

Fila's response has stood unchallenged since that very night. His response was that the subject performing judgment about beauty or effectiveness is subject to the same difficulties noted at the first step, when the subject first encounters the object of knowledge: the problem of how to tell the difference between the subject and the object, i.e., how to avoid bias, which requires conflict and controversy, and can't possibly be simple recognition of knowledge from wherever or, more relevant, whenever it comes. That would go beyond Plato's wildest fever memory dreams, to require that every individual human mind already contains all knowledge from all times, with no amnesia, and that would render history and therefore individual subjective activity meaningless. This object may require that method, and it is not that there must be no change in the subject, and it is not like there must be no history to mind, subject, or thought. Fila's position never demanded, required, or postulated the immediate infinitude of the individual subject, just the eventual universality of subjective activity, i.e., reason—which must occur across individual lifespans because science is a social endeavor— and the eventual adequacy of the subject, i.e., the collective human subject, to the ultimate object, infinite knowledge. Which means we must now and always be quite jealous, on behalf of the object, of the space between us and it.

Fila hoped that the debate would turn toward questions of how individuals would or could participate in such a boundless wonder, but he concluded pointedly against any sort of reliance on recognition or remembrance where reason can still perform. We must not presume to be able to recognize knowledge from different places and times. Recognition may well be that of old prejudices or faulty knowledge, and so the principles derived would be those judged beautiful or effective by those with that prejudice or faulty knowledge. The so-called practical position pretends to avoid philosophical questions of subjectivity, mind and knowledge at one stage, demagogically dismissing them as concerns of abstract principle, while merely reintroducing those same philosophical problems later at the moment of judgment, where they are uglier and even more vulgar, begging arguments about the utility of this or that bit of learning in these or those terms while dancing on the head of a pin. And after that, well, things really get bad.

While positions have hardened, and there is little direct engagement anymore, that second controversy remained unresolved.

◆ ◆ ◆

In any case, when Fila was in the castle, Prince Appall had charged his own chancellery with the maintenance of the church registry, but upon his discharge that responsibility reverted back to Fila. Fila managed things fine the first two years after the war, but he started to slip after the growth of the new thing with Tellem. One fine afternoon in September 2133, the prince felt it necessary to gather some of his young wards—Rytius, Ritius, Balloony Louis, and Milkman Washington—arm them with swords, and send them to investigate and to correct matters at the offices of the church registry. Fila had failed to send in several months of records and accompanying revenues from collections. They were hardly more than boys eager to prove their mettle. Rytius is the one who kept it civilized, and he and a grateful Fila became friends. Fila was the big brother Rytius never had, and wished he could be.

GJ and Sugarpie and Huggums and Koleeko

The nave of St. Mark's was cold and empty, but the annex housing Fila's Finds was warmly lit against the sunless morning. Rytius could see the figure of his friends moving distorted through the fine stained glass window in the door. The skittering of the freezing drizzle seemed to rush and drag behind the rhythm it played against the windows, a popcorn rattle echo, never matching the taps on his back.

"Rytius," his friend greeted him through the door. He opened it. "You're a little early."

"Now, you know I'm coming to help set up," Rytius smiled and stepped across the threshold. "Break down, too." It was warm inside and the air was spiced with fruitwood smoke. Fila Green, the first record-keeper, was having breakfast with his wife Carnation, at the table, by the window, next to the wood furnace.

"What are you doing? Get in here," rushed Carnation. "And close that door!" Rytius hustled in and threw his coat over the deer skull and antlers on the wall. Carnation had made a coat rack of sanded driftwood and some oversized hand-wrought galvanized nails she bought from D-Man, and she had placed it right near the door, but there was something special about the skull. No one used the rack until the head and all the antlers were full.

Rytius held his tongue and was patient as Carnation got in his business, encouraging him to go out with Vinilla or Bonbon or Xena or Tracey, and he cherished his friends with special greetings, pouring himself a cup of coffee, seating himself, brewing another pot, and refilling their cups. Rytius began to wonder whether his patience was not actually cowardice, and he turned words over in his mind to come up with the right ones to tell Fila and Carnation about the prince's tower, and then he wondered whether he should wait until after the ceremony, because this was their daughter's naming day. And then Sugarpie and GJ arrived.

George Jefferson Wallace, a refugee from Brooklyn before the war, was a couple of years older than Fila. Born to the game, he had always kept his own records in stories and music. He was their living link to the recordkeepers of New York, who mostly lived in Brooklyn and the Bronx, often facilitating trades between them and those of New Ark. Even in New York he had made his living as a painter of houses and a decorator of walls, an artist of a sort with a curious geometric style, making his own pigments from stones, plants, and various chemical compounds. He did the same in New Ark.

Sugarpie Freeman was a Newark native but was orphaned in the war at 11. She ran with a gang of street children for a year and a half until she was arrested with some others from her gang in a bakery after hours. The policeman cited the girls for solicitation, knowing full well that they had only been stealing. That set them up for the convict trade, and Sugarpie was set to be sent down to Atlantic City, then still dominated by a ruthless Dominion mafia fending off the attacks of the Illadelph Lunatix on its drug dealers, casinos and brothels. The Dominion representative and his van of convicted accountants, plumbers and electricians was kidnapped in transit, and did not arrive to complete the prisoner swap, and so she was conscripted to an industrial hemp farm near Berlin, in southern New Jersey. An old Gardener family named Mead owned the farm, but slowly lost it to debts incurred to the Omega Detachment over the next 5 years. They encouraged the Meads to borrow against their property to contract for a new roof, to purchase new tractors, and to install a custom-built irrigation system. She was among a group of convict laborers who took off on foot through the forests the night before the foreclosure, but they split up at Lake Pine, where some went south to maroon at Wildwood, where the Belleplain forest would protect them from assaults over land, and others headed east to the piers at Tom's River, hoping to catch a ship bound south for the Dominion, and the rest, including Sugarpie, followed Wharton forest trails to Princeton and points north, back to Newark and New York. But she had learned all that there is to learn about weaving bast fibers.

She and GJ joined forces to manufacture and dye their own textiles, which were prized for their quality, pattern, and color, and they married soon after that. GJ had a good 15 years on Sugarpie, and so he had some business cards printed:

If an old man loves a young woman, that's his business.
And if a young woman loves an old man, that's her business.
If they decide to get married, that's their business.
If you turn this card over, that's *our* business.

Sugarpie was provocative, and GJ was subtle in gameplay. Together they were masterful, each playing to the other's strength. They played one another in the oldest continuous game, rooted in Sugarpie's long-ago kickoff of the Comedy Games, and they often polled colleagues, recruiting them to join one side or the other of this game, conducted by means of posing subtly variant thought experiments constructed to highlight aspects of the question of the exhaustion or renewal of the blues legacy of the olden United States by the turn of the twenty-first century.

GJ was for the exhaustion, and Sugarpie defended first continuity and then renewal. They even wove it into their fabric, different approaches to pattern and color identifying their opposing perspectives, and they treated it as though it had dispositive implications for literally every other game played in those days. If GJ was right, and the blues legacy had been exhausted by the end of the Nixon Administration, then the relevance of various records created after the exhaustion would need serious devaluation.

Exacting recordkeepers assuming continuity between, say, 1968 and 2000 would be horrified to have to discount many folk classics, from "Rock the Bells" to "black owned," and the records indeed showed resistance to that discounting, even in those days, when folks staunchly defended whatever blues-based artists managed to produce. If Sugarpie was right, and the musical flowering of the late twentieth century was a revival and not a last gasp, then the relevance of records created after this renaissance would need serious revaluation. Naïve recordkeepers would have misunderstood new subjectivities politicking or making art with new powers in a new freedom. Sugarpie came to understand that assuming continuity between, say, 1948 and 2000 would be to abandon the search for these lost new notions of freedom, as propounded perhaps by her favorite historical avatars Queen Latifah and President Barack Obama. For Sugarpie, they were signs of renewal. To treat work produced in the early 1950s the same as work produced in the 1990s would be to ignore the radical change in concrete life possibilities over that time. Freedom itself would need to be made an object of any inquiry into its effect on the art produced. This was provocation, indeed, because it sounded like allowing different standards for art, depending on the marketing, which is a rotten kettle of fish best left unopened. Their duel had dark implications for most games in those days, and they proceeded in spite of the social effect of their debate. It gathered and built, piled and darkened like a summer cumulus, shading all proceedings below.

They hustled in—the raindrops had grown too large to freeze in the air—and GJ took Sugarpie's coat before he took off his own, and he stood looking wondering whether to use the antlers or the hook. He chose an antler for her coat and the hook for his own.

GJ reached into the inside pocket of the coat he had just hung up, and withdrew three saddle-stitched octavos.

He took his seat and slid one copy of each to Fila, Carnation, and Rytius.

"What's this?" asked Fila, superfluously, reading the title.

Shady and the Soul Stealers

by

G.J. Wallace

"You finished? Congratulations!" Fila jumped up and embraced him.

GJ grinned from ear to ear. "Thank you, Fila. You know it's been a long time coming."

Carnation clapped. "Oh, my goodness, I can't wait to read it."

"This looks amazing," Rytius added. "I mean the book looks great." It was pressed on a thin cream-colored paper, with a beautiful purple-black ink. He flipped it over to read the back cover blurb.

> *His acts are the hottest, his woman is the baddest, and his lifestyle is the finest.*
>
> At the turn of the twenty-first century, Houston, Texas, music mogul Peter "Shady" Cross, C.E.O. of Axe-'Em Records, takes the hip-hop world by storm, with hardcore acts from the Bayou City, like the Head Cutters, the Flood Pushers, and the Fifth Ward Trap Dawgs, but also cutting-edge lyricists like the Sinaesthetics and the conscious and progressive Sugarland Plan Station.
>
> But he has a soft side. He discovers, signs and produces Tanasia Bellfort, *a k a* Bella Bodaccio, who rises to the top of the soul and r&b charts.
>
> She also steals his heart.

But everything changes when his old friend Martin Milkie comes back to town with questions about Pete's past…a studio fire destroys Axe-'Em's unreleased master tapes, and Bella disappears without a trace…

"It ain't what you don't know that gets you into trouble. It's what you know for sure that just ain't so." —Mark Twain

"I can't wait to read it either," Rytius agreed.

"You all know Huggums, right?" Sugarpie asked, pulling her chair closer to GJ, pulling his right arm around her shoulder.

"Huggums Dearly? Who makes those little gyroscope toys? He lives in Brookside," Rytius answered. "With his girlfriend, Koleeko."

"Jensen. Koleeko Jensen. I know her auntie, May Bee," said Carnation. "She made me a basket."

"I saw him getting breakfast a couple days ago, near that market over there," Fila added. "Right around the corner from you, Rytius."

"Yeah, well, that's the spot," Rytius said. He sold duck eggs to Skyfire Adams at least once a week, and sometimes more. She ran a dairy stand at one of a couple of usual spots in the arcade, and he sold her cider for various holidays. Sometimes all the vendors couldn't fit into the space, and they spilled out up and down the street. The prince had given up trying to lease spots because anybody who had enough money for a store would get one. It would be stupid to waste money renting a stall in a street market. So the rule was first come, first reserved. You move, you lose.

"Well," Sugarpie began, leaning in. "Yesterday he came home from the market and he was mad about getting cheated out of money, like with counterfeit coins. Copper-plated zinc instead of copper, and silver-plated steel instead of silver. She asked him who cheated him and he said 'everybody,' and he started crying, so she started trying to calm him down, right? So she gets him sitting down and she wants to find out names so she can get the police or at least the market security. He won't tell her who, because he says they'll kill him, because they've been cheating him for years, and he wasn't ever supposed to find out. She started getting scared, but she kept on trying to keep him calm. He jumped up and ran to get the money to show her, 'cause he started talking about how if she didn't believe him he would show her. He got them, and she looked but it was copper and silver. He fell on the floor laughing, talking about how somebody switched it back."

"Oh, no," Fila moaned. Carnation sighed. GJ sat silently, and began to roll a marijuana cigarette in the old double-twist style, with thin paper. "Anybody want one?" he asked. "I have tobacco, too." "I'll take one of those," Fila said. Sugarpie grew both plants herself.

"Yes. But then he stopped laughing and started crying again. I don't know how well you know Koleeko, but she's trying to stay calm and just figure out what in God's creation must have happened, because he can't be so upset about the money because the money can't be the problem, right? It's got to be something else. She starts trying to find out what set him off, but he keeps going on about how he wants to move somewhere else, he wants them out now, tonight, and she's trying to think up who might have made him so mad and she showed him the coins again and said they're real, you know what I mean? Like just look and you can see. He knocked the coins out of her hand—I mean all over the room—he hit her hand so hard he broke her pinky—and started talking about how they have to leave right now, tonight. She tried to hug him and get him to sit down on the sofa, but he pushed her on the sofa and wouldn't let her get up, trying to make her answer if she was going to leave with him or not. She said she would, and she said he had to let her get up if he wanted her to pack and he fell down laughing again, and he said he was sorry, and he was on the floor crying and laughing, so she got up and ran into the bedroom and locked the door. He started accusing her of helping them to cheat him, and kicking on the bedroom door. She started screaming out the window for somebody to go get a police."

"Oh, my God," said Carnation, mouth agape.

Rytius drawled a wordless horror. GJ finished twisting his joint and set it down, unlit. He drew a mechanical finger roller and some wadded filter cotton from a pants pocket to complete Fila's tobacco cigarette.

"Yes. Somebody did go get a police, and it was three of them as a matter of fact. Huggums wouldn't open the front door and he was still shouting and beating on the door inside so they kicked in the door and took him out."

"Where is he now?" asked Fila, taking the tobacco cigarette from GJ and putting it in his breast pocket. GJ likewise stashed his joint. Rytius wanted to ask for one now, but it was too late. Besides, he was already, still, a little drunk.

"They've got him in the jail infirmary," Sugarpie said. "They charged him with assault and battery on Koleeko *and* one of the officers."

"We should go see him," suggested Carnation, and of course everyone agreed.

"How is Koleeko?" Rytius asked.

"Devastated. How you think?" Sugarpie answered.

Thus deprived of light conversation and unsure what to do or how to help, it wasn't long before the five colleagues moved to the nave to finish the decorations before everyone else arrived.

Cartesia Boniface

She awoke naturally to the muted thumps of rain on her double-paned bay windows high above the street, and slowly stretched her arm out to caress Lee's side, all the while knowing that she would not be there. Lee only slept over Saturday nights into Sunday mornings, working all the others. Cartesia had asked her twice to let her take care of her, and she would not ask again. She had tried to reason with Lee. Lee and her friend Tee had kept in good touch with their old baby sisters-in-law, and Cartesia had ensured that they had made good impressions upon the princes—they were already partners. She pulled her arms back to her sides, hugged herself and admitted that she had not reasoned but that she had shamelessly pleaded and begged. Thereafter Cartesia had begun to feel endangered, as though she were holding herself carelessly open. She had caught herself searching Lee's face for signs of strain or deceit, perhaps in the form of averted eyes or a stolen glance, and she had felt ashamed when their eyes met last night, and Lee's face lit up, and her own breath quickened when she saw Lee seeing what Lee saw in her. She knew that Lee could never betray her, because she wielded state power, and she knew that Lee loved her, in her own way. And likewise.

She had shared her bed with beautiful and powerful men and beautiful, powerful men, the best of whom had wanted nothing more than for her to love him as he loved her. In her youth she had believed that such a thing were possible and even desirable, but her long experience tending that delicate flower had taught her that one must always be loved more than one loves, and that any man who thinks otherwise is a fool, born to be treated rough and made to like it. For a man to claim to want nothing more than to share a life and a love, nothing more than to be valued as he values, is to admit that he has nothing of superior value to offer. Possessed of any treasure worth having, he would resist such encroachments, demand gestures of submission, and tend more to the withholding of his affections.

Her first had left her his Lincoln Park fortress and his security services operation, which was the first licensed to police New Ark's markets and stores. Since Appall's death, its operation had been restricted to Feelharmonica's principality. Her second bequeathed her his scholarly library and his land holdings in the Great Swamp. She made use of the former.

Each in his own way had failed her. Each had debased and humiliated himself in his eagerness to love her, and both had demeaned themselves in pursuit of her love. Their bequeathals, gifts, and concessions were the smallest of consolations, the coldest of comforts. But she had learned to take that comfort in that coldness.

And so she tended to strike fear into the hearts of those around her, men and women alike.

◆ ◆ ◆

A sort of all-purpose executrix from Piscataway, who also happened to be the daughter of a large landowner there, Cartesia Boniface had first made a career as an assistant prosecutor for Appall, then chief prosecutor, then jurist under Feelharmonica, then also councilor and jurist, during which time she also managed to raise two children, bury two husbands, and publish several well-respected articles on the major part of her work: criminal psychology and related practical applications. Her work in that field, though written in a crabbed, sui generis "academic" style, surpassed that of any recordkeeper in insight and understanding. Tellem underwrote a non-exclusionary dig through his collection in search of criminology records confirming or denying the work of the Councilor Justice Cartesia Boniface.

There is no doubt that she was useful to the state and to the prince, particularly Appall, where she crafted Appall's legal strategy for domestic pacification, in which political dissidents were prosecuted under a set of guidelines, not laws, under which crimes against the state and the prince (defined elsewhere, in law) were divided into vague and fuzzy bands, to which clouds of fog were assigned explicit and harsh minimum punishments. The circumstances of the deaths of her husbands have always been disputed, and obscured by loss and mishandling of important evidence in each case. Let the obvious be stated, that the Black Lady was everywhere assumed to have killed them, and there is no way that she could not have known this. Her children from her first two husbands had grown, and while she remained capable of bearing children, and while she appeared only to grow in beauty, no third man submitted a bid for her hand.

She made great use of the criminology research with which Tellem's team had provided her, particularly the criminal use of psychology in the Americas of the early twenty-first century. Organized crime concerns, including governments in whole or in part, concurred on the use of the particularly effective tactic of social isolation to heighten and then to exploit the emotional reactivity of suspects or targets, depending. These tactics, reinforced by easy control of the electronic communications infrastructure prevalent in those societies, served a strategy of self-destruction—to encourage the targets or suspects to destroy themselves, to alienate themselves from their own support systems, families, friends, etc., and eventually to break under the strain. Of course, this is an uncertain strategy, and in certain cases more forceful tactics were required, including the surreptitious administration of mind-altering substances capable of inducing alarming states of conciousness in which the target or suspect might seem capable of harming themselves or others, which would then require conveniently lethal self-defense from well-placed operatives or at least involuntary restraint by law enforcement. Their testimony is thereby also pre-emptively impeached.

Her main takeaway was that recalcitrant cases could be eliminated or incapacitated to a greater or lesser degree more or less easily depending on their addictions, habits, and predilections. The more exotic, perverse, and distasteful the better. If there were no such vulnerabilities, well, then, one could surreptitiously administer other types of substances.

Who would know? Who *could* know? If there was one thing she herself knew, it was that dead men tell no tales.

Naming

Naming is a matter of ultimate concern, and while there is neither accepted liturgy nor tradition, the ceremony is fired by the same holy spirit as that which descended upon the apostles on the first Pentecost. The church was indeed the proper place for the ceremony, but neither Fila nor Carnation thought a preacher was appropriate. So, the pulpit was empty, and Fila stood on the floor below, in front of the friends and family gathered in the pews. Fila was from a long line of preachers, and though he was not one himself, and while he had notions perhaps different from those of his forefathers, he would never do anything capable of being misconstrued as sacrilegious. And seeing as how he ran the church registry, if he were to disrespect himself or the Lord's house in that manner, he might not hear any rebukes directly to his face, but he would swim, backbit, for who knows how long, in a dark sea of rumors, gossip, and all the flotsam and jetsam of resentment and unaired grievance.

But Fila was indeed from a long line of preachers.

◆ ◆ ◆

Fila made a scene when he entered the nave from the hallway leading to the pastor's office, the conference room, and, down at the end of the hallway, the industrial kitchen, which had a door on its adjacent wall into the church annex (including the breakfast nook by the window), the original site of Fila's Finds. The perpetually somehow misaligned swinging door swung open freely, but closed crazily, sometimes only halfway before bouncing and clattering back closed, eventually pumping down to rattle against the outer edge of the frame, but for two separate and sometimes counteracting, sometimes reinforcing reasons: the first was the hydraulic damper, which had been replaced numerous times, but which kept failing in the exact same manner for the second reason, which was that the foundation of the building was cracked, and Fila maintained that it was entirely stable, not having deteriorated in years, but that meant that the doorframe was bent, and Pastor Snap Arnold, who was shortly to receive a ricochet bounce off his buddy BB's belly and onto the wall, had frequently joked that their cursed door might be some new kind of miracle of the Adversary, but told all gathered that no one should mention his joke. So Fila fairly jumped out of the doorway, to the side, clearing any danger zone where the door might swing back, bounce, or stop surprisingly, but he also slamming into the back of a recordkeeper named Bubble Bee Vernon from Nanuet who made the trip for Fila's daughter special and that was not an entirely safe and routine journey as a matter of course.

"BB, you seen Rob?" Fila asked. BB had not. Fila helped Pastor Arnold to his feet, and turned on his heels, stepping to the nearest of his comrades, friends, and colleagues who may not have overheard. That nearest was one of Tellem's historians, an extremely tall recordkeeper named Voom Ipcress from Englewood, a childhood refugee from the first Saint Patrick's Day massacre whose parents wanted nothing to do with the Gardeners, but preferred even to die staying and fighting for their place in New Ark, whatever that was going to be.

"You seen him?"

"I haven't the foggiest…" Voom began.

"Rob! From the Bronx?"

"Oh, yeah. I saw him a second ago. I think he said something about going to get something, and I have the impression he thought it was on his bike?"

"But you definitely saw him?"

"Absolutely. Liz? You saw Rob, right?"

Voom turned to Elizabeth Jones, one of the youngest of Tellem's faction. She would call herself a mere apprentice, but she had been on teams responsible for exclusions in autoimmune disease, specifically any CRISPR-induced cancer epidemic, and agronomy, specifically any situation in which excess rainfall leached critical levels of minerals and eroded sufficient fertile soil to cause famine in breadbasket regions.

"I haven't seen him at all. But why are you asking us? See, where is she…"

Elizabeth tiptoed to look around to see "Dancy! There she is."

Elizabeth fell back to her heels and bounced aloft once more. "Dancy! Dancy! Come on over here! Fila need to talk to you!" she shrieked wincingly wildly, like a heathen.

"She's coming," Elizabeth announced, pleased and proud. Dancy Ricardo was a supremely talented recordkeeper born and raised in New Ark. Her gameplay was a model to all her peers and many elders besides, because she had a way of looping back over pieces of her material to reveal new aspects of things that neither she nor the group had noticed the first time. She began to play with the shapes of these rediscoveries, to form higher-level constructs with the elements looped over, play them against one another and start new cycles of repetition and discovery. This was sufficient for a young recordkeeper to earn honor and praise, but what made Dancy special, and her talent undeniable, was her discipline. No listener at any of her presentations had ever had the slightest suspicion that they were being toyed with, that formal tricks had been sought and imposed, that the player had some sort of card up their sleeve. These are not mere impressions, but ways of knowing that communication has been compromised, whereas if recordkeeping may be said to have an ethic it is integrity in communication, in order to preserve the possibility of communion with the past. Her rediscoveries were genuine and material. Colleagues traded flowcharts of her presentations, and it was a matter of some discord whether her listeners should be writing so much during her presentations, and shouldn't they rather be participating. Recordkeepers should never be mere scribes, no matter how brilliant the speaker.

Fila smiled as she approached. "My lil' ol' baby sis!" He hugged her and she play-choked before he bent down so that she could kiss him on the cheek. She hugged him around his midsection after he stood back upright. She was not a tall young woman.

"I'm looking for your man, Rob," Fila smiled down at her.

"I don't know where that man went," she said. "He told me he had put my present in the basket and I asked him before we even left and he still didn't do it. He said he forgot something on the bike, but I think he just went home to go get it."

"Just now he left?"

"No, I ain't seen him since we got here 'cause I was helping set up the food, right?"

"Well, yeah, but Liz said…"

"No, I just saw him, Dancy," said Voom.

"So he came back? Already?" Fila asked someone.

"I don't know," Dancy admitted.

"I know I just saw him. He'll be back," said Voom. "What's the problem, anyway?"

"He's got something I need for the ceremony," Fila replied.

"You let Rob hold something for which you have a time-sensitive mission-critical need?" asked Dancy.

"Yeah," Fila laughed. "I guess I might as well make my way on up to the front."

◆ ◆ ◆

"I need to see somebody one time, wait a minute," Fila said, loudly, his voice booming over and across the din of gentle conversation amid the pews as he struggled and squeezed his way to the front of the aisle. He did not mount the podium nor even climb the stairs but when he reached the end of the aisle he merely turned on the floor and asked somebody, anybody, if they had please seen Rob? Nickname Sinclair? You know, Rob, from the Bronx?

"Where is that man at, 'cause I know I saw him earlier." Fila knew how to hold a crowd on the edge of whether this truly was a general announcement, or whether they owed him deference anyway because he was the host, or whether they should ignore him now, or whether he had finally lost his entire mind. "See, you all don't understand," he started again, letting everyone within his rather wide earshot knew they were being addressed. He was indeed the host. "I need to talk to Rob for my baby girl's naming ceremony." There was a beautiful harmony of various gapemouthed subvocalizations as understanding descending among those gathered. They asked their neighbors and none among them seemed to have seen him and first the rumor of consensus and then the consensus rumor floated slowly, at higher and more decisive volumes, toward Fila, who, of course, had heard the entire development.

"No, no, you all still don't understand. Here he goes now," Fila said, pointing back toward the entrance, in which Robert Upton Sirius stood, grinning.

"I made it, boss!" he yelled. This was hilarious for some reason and it was not the first time laughter had raised the roof of that building, but it was one of not many.

"Oh, good, now we can start," Fila announced, calling the audience's attention back to the front, whereupon he pulled a face, as though to ask them to get a load of this guy. "But it's true, though. I need my man Rob here today because you found a story you wanted to tell, right, Rob?"

"A story?" Rob asked, from way back at the door.

"Well, it's more of a joke. You copied it out yourself, remember?"

"Oh, uh," Rob mugged himself, pulling his pockets inside out, checking his woolens, patting himself down. "Oh, Fila, man, I'm so sorry," Rob apologized.

"Rob? You forgot it? Today of all days?" Fila asked. Heads swiveled back to the front for the response.

Rob just stood there hangdog. "I'm sorry, man." He was a standup fellow, all told, to apologize to his friend, whom he had let down, in front of everyone. Everyone turned back to see what Fila would say next.

"Sorry? You're sorry?" Fila yelled. "Are you serious?"

Rob stood still for a moment, looking even sadder than before. His head hung even lower than it had. Folks started feeling bad for him, and Fila beating up on the poor boy. And then he lifted his head, and coughed, and then he said, "No, Fila. I'm…I'm…I'm Betelgeuse."

The sympathy his public apology had purchased was displaced by revulsion at nonsense when words of honor were required. They all turned back, feeling betrayed, to Fila, whose wrath upon Rob they would welcome. And Fila stood there stonefaced. He looked from face to face, and as he did, he could not help but let his expression soften, and his features spread into one of the widest grins he had ever grinned and doubled himself over with his guffawing, and everybody got the joke of course. But they were still a little mad, though. And that's why Fila started quickly.

"I wanted to take it back to elementary school for a minute. You all know that dumb joke. Now, did you know, that my man Rob—thank you, Rob—Rob goes by Sinclair, and that's how a lot of you know him, because his middle name was Upton, so it's a play on that oldenday author's name. So you might not know that he went around with that joke, 'R.U. Sirius', as a name for a long time, and he was doing that when I met him. He was a smart boy, though, and he gave himself real middle names for the initials. And that's what lets him go by Sinclair now. He changed his name. And you know why he did it. That's the whole thing, really. To say it clearly, when you meet a man like this," he pointed to Rob, who had taken his place next to Dancy, "you know, with the cantaloupe head and the jughandle ears, right," he mocked Rob for a laugh.

Rob was a sport, of course. "I KNOW YOU DIDN'T MENTION HEAD SHAPE," Rob barked back.

"Oh, right, true. My bad, Rob. My point is, when you meet a man like that, and you hear that name 'R.U. Sirius', well, you know right away. You know right away you're dealing with someone capable of acting a God damned fool. You will never be disappointed at the man or woman behind a name, because of a name, ever again. You know right away that you are talking to…to what?" he asked the gathering.

He answered, "*a child*. Really, you can't ever forget it. But as they grow older, what is it they are growing into? Is it the foolishness, the silliness of the name they chose? No. It's the beginning of wisdom when they understand why we do it like this. They realize how foolish it was to grant a child the right to name the adult. But then in that moment, they recognize the honor, respect, and credit we gave that child, for no other reason than that child said they were ready to join us. In the next moment, that child, now a grown man or woman, realizes that nothing has really changed, and that it would always have been that way. There are no rules on the name the child chooses when they join the community of those who must be addressed, here, in public, where we stand naked, alone, frightened, here, where we must speak and make ourselves heard. We need them to join us, because we need them to help us, and we always did, oldendays and nowadays. What rules could prevent the growth of monsters? The child names the adult so that the adult remembers. That remembrance is the fulfillment of the promise to remember. That promise is simply the *right* of the child to name the adult. And that's new. That's special. Never before has this humility found actual material practice in secular tradition. Let me say that plain again. The self-creation that we celebrate here today is also an eternal public display of childishness. We use it to remember. To remember that we grownups, we're scared too. We're not ready, either. Still. We are no more ready now than we were then. But here we stand, each of us giving what we were given, and what we must by now know we surely didn't deserve: the benefit of the doubt."

With that Fila invited his daughter up to introduce herself, in her own words, on her own terms, with her own name.

Castle Henderson

There had been no incident of any kind. The bed of the black truck was filled, and rents in coin and kind shifting heaved—canvas bags stuffed with envelopes of silver, gold and copper jangled against uneaten winter stores of potatoes and southern-bought grains, which would serve as starches for alms and cakes for Saint Patrick's Day. Among the sacks of grain and money were carefully lain boxes of distilled spirits, their glass bottles separated by heavy paper shocks, rattling nonetheless, neck against uneven neck, because the boxes had not been properly fully filled. Ritius had long ago recognized a sort of rise and fall where rents were concerned. When he first began these duties, the fall in the quantity and value of the rents after the first autumn month would enrage him, driving him excessively to punish both debtors and those who offered moonshine instead of money. The knowledge that the people's wealth was more like the seasons, and that one may as well reprimand the sea for waving, made him feel wise and merciful. He was no fool, though, and he still wouldn't accept wine, cider, or beer. The quality is too various, and the temptations of the job had made it impossible to find sober, reliable inspectors to regulate the production of the entire universe of fermented alcoholic beverages.

◆ ◆ ◆

Ritius wished to speak with Prince Feelharmonica about more than the rise and fall of the rents. He had to wait outside the office, because Feelharmonica was meeting with the spy he had engaged to surveil his older brother to the south, Prince Koolkup of New Gunswick. According to Ritius, Feelharmonica was making a mountain out of a molehill, and the molehill was Koolkup's management of his relationship with New York, regarding Staten Island. There remained one single bridge connecting Staten Island to New Jersey, and it was hard to overestimate its economic and political significance, as it was both an explicit condition of the peace between North New Jersey and New York, and the source of the only, though great and growing, import tax revenue Koolkup received, and his principality was the bulwark against the chaos of southern New Jersey. So he took frequent trips to New York, spoke most frequently with New York, and had business relations with many Staten Island merchants and factors and tradesmen and the like.

◆ ◆ ◆

There were three concubines in Feelharmonica's parlor. Sorrel, his favorite, dared to stay when Ritius entered. Ritius determined to ignore her entirely. Feelharmonica considered himself to be open-minded and liberal in his relations with his women, and Sorrel had grown comfortable in her role as a sort of secret streetwise counselor. Feelharmonica believed that he could use her while properly discounting her distorted partial perspective and any ill will she might harbor against him for her position. She was well compensated after all, and she did not desire to be his wife—he did not feel he needed one, yet—and she would not have desired children even if she were capable of it. Ritius had told him more than once that he relied too much on her, which is to say, at all. But Feelharmonica was proud to possess a woman of her intellectual acuity. He enjoyed her little games, and was confident that he had them well in hand. She was quite well placed, and had come to know everyone of any note. "I swear to you, Ritius, that Koolkup is going to be THE RUIN OF OUR KINGDOM," Feelharmonica pronounced, seating himself informally on the sofa. Sorrel took his side and curled and shifted her legs under herself like a cat. It was some small relief to Ritius that Feelharmonica dismissed her before she had gotten entirely comfortable. The prince enjoyed his little games as well.

Ritius took the club chair across from him and poured them both a bit of whisky.

"Can I be honest for a minute?" Ritius asked, while sliding the prince's drink across.

"I don't know," Feelharmonica grinned. "Can you?" He took a sip and sucked his teeth.

"That so-called covenant? established something, but it surely wasn't a kingdom."

"Not this double-dug dirt again," Feelharmonica groaned. "I'm about to start taking it the wrong way."

"You have yet to dispute my logic?" Ritius felt that, as a soldier and as a servant, he had to reiterate his position. "This were a kingdom only had your father survived."

The Covenant established a sovereignty of some sort under the name of New Ark, but it was really just a treaty, and no founding document. There was discussion neither of the sovereign's border with southern New Jersey nor its administrative or executive structure, nor its inner divisions or succession policy. The only geographical discussion was the explicit confirmation that Staten Island indeed still belonged to New York. Prince Appall ignored all these questions of state. His only condition, spoken, was that New Ark, the middle portion of the sovereignty, would be *primus inter pares*.

"But still. You remain *primo enterprise*. So if there's anyone in a position to finally found that kingdom? it remains you."

Feelharmonica glared at Ritius. He remembered when they met, long ago, in this, his father's very house. Ritius was a bit older, months, and Feelharmonica and his younger brother (before he took the name Razorbeem) played with all the children of the house—his mother's sisters' daughters and his father's wards, pages, and squires—and these two, Feelharmonica and Ritius, were boyhood friends for as long as Prince Appall would allow. Feelharmonica came of age, and he grew to learn his father's callousness, particularly toward his very own self, as he, in his heart, abandoned his boyhood friend to his fate as his servant. His father died before teaching him the most salient method of converting pride and self-regard into a chrysalis of contempt, so that he might cope with such crippling isolation.

◆ ◆ ◆

That frightful alchemy almost always entails the systematic abuse and humiliation of those one wishes to dominate, but only because at the end of such treatment, the dominated, now deprived of their dignity, cry out for further insult, and can in no way appear similar to oneself. For instance, there was nothing natural about the way in which the Coleman boys came to Castle Henderson, though such a thing might be expected, given the status and position of the people involved.

Fastes Coleman was a military leader, like his father before him, and his before him. He was Appall's favorite of his father's armorbearers, as it had been with Feelharmonica and Ritius. So, at the beginning of his reign, Appall appointed Fastes general of the legion he raised against the south, to establish and fortify his brother Boy at Trenton, where he would be a sort of marshal over the territory, and also necessarily to push the Gardeners back up against the Virginian Dominion, in hopes that the Gardeners would be crushed and die out, abandoned, exiled, and mercilessly extorted by the marauding paramilitaries of the long demobilized and disbanded Pennsylvania National Guard, who were more properly called Illadelphians then, rather than now, after discord and strife have split them apart; they remain what they were, only with smaller forces and that many more enemies.

Fastes performed his duties for 7 years.

Appall was and had always been generous to Fastes, his trusted general, calling him a friend. No one could recall Fastes ever trading upon his familiarity with the prince, and Fastes never made any attempt to challenge Appall publicly on any matter of state. It might be said that Fastes retreated too abruptly into private life. He and his new wife Lalala—a dressmaker originally from Roosevelt, Long Island—eloped and honeymooned the springtime with her people, conceiving their first child, the boy who named himself Rytius. By no accounts was Appall at all shaken by this. He spoke with no one about his friend, General Fastes, and in fact, Appall hosted a celebration for the newlyweds upon their return from Long Island.

Appall praised Lalala for her poise, because she was a common woman. He did not mention what no one failed to notice. Her beauty was such that a man would stop walking, talking and breathing just to watch her move across the room. Her body was thoroughbred perfection, and her eyes betrayed secret wonders of thought and feeling a man might do wicked things to know.

But Appall and Fastes embraced one another, laughed together, danced with one another's wives, and generally played fools that evening.

Appall had not yet hardened his heart against his old friend. Or perhaps he was practicing the duplicity that later served him so well.

He did bark Fastes whether it were a greater honor to have a prince attend a wedding, to have a prince host a wedding, or to have a prince miss a wedding. The outburst struck everyone silent. Even the piano player stopped. Fastes paused, smiled and barked that the last option is the best, because one can be sure that the prince, having missed one opportunity to show off, is sure to make an even grander display of generosity. The hall exploded in laughter, Appall actually fell off his chair, and when Fastes went to him, he also fell, and they tumbled down drunk, laughing.

Appall did not fail to govern, and early the next March, he again took up arms against rebels in the north, who began calling themselves Gardeners after those in the south. Appall raised a brigade, naming it after Saint Patrick, and its policy was to wipe these New Gardeners from the face of the earth or, failing that, to push them south of Trenton. The Gardeners, new or old, had no policy, because they had neither king nor prince nor ruler of any kind, but they are loosely bound by their ideas of liberty and justice. Their ideas and their flag are heirlooms, but they are like their forefathers who somehow never managed to live in the manner they preached. They, like their forefathers, are as poisonous as the snake they hold aloft, always carrying in their mouths a ready excuse for unfreedom, false imprisonment and injustice. But they were more than capable of bombing bridges and sabotaging dams as they fled southwest into the forests and swamps.

Appall soon required a team of builders, craftsmen and engineers of several kinds to inspect and to renovate the three dams near Paterson, and to restore the electrical power supply, if possible. The Passaic flows north for a while, from out of the swamps of County Morris, to the Little Falls dam near the Great Notch in the Achtung Mountains, and north still to the Great Falls dam at Paterson, just north of which the water turns south, toward the ocean again, to Dundee dam, near the town of Garfield, and thence the river runs down the plains to New Ark and the bay. All this territory was occupied by New Gardeners, and that team of highly skilled men, though under armed protection, suffered casualties sufficient to raise alarm, and so Appall commanded Fastes to take a small squadron to the Great Notch, while Fastes's firstborn child was not yet three months old.

If a stream of southernbound refugees forms a river, Appall sent Fastes and his squadron swimming upstream, north along the western face of Orange Mountain. No one survived, and Appall took Lalala and her infant son into his home, where they lived under his protection. That December she bore him a son.

Perhaps a year after the birth of that second son, the boy who would name himself Ritius, Lalala fell ill with raving. She was found wandering Brookside, near House Coleman, half-naked, her face garishly painted, as though she were a sorceress or a clown or both, ranting about debt and recompense, not vacating the throne nor ever abandoning the castle but reinforcing the fastness, and Appall formed a bodyguard for her, and brought doctors to look after her health. She told visitors that she was the sovereign, and that Appall was not even a pretender but a worm eating around the edges of her seat, spoiling her place, biting and stinging her behind. He began to confine her to her rooms when appropriate, and then regularly, as a matter of course. After she overturned a heavily laden dinner table one evening, Appall began to consider her a danger to herself and others. When required, he did not hesitate to strap her down to her bed. Her guards became jailers, and soon she had no visitors save Appall, two nights a week, three weeks per month.

She never withered, but she threw herself out of her bedroom window one morning when her guard released her for breakfast. Appall's associates had forgotten her, and he did not proclaim her death. There was no record of the younger child's true paternity, and upon their official conscription into his service, the boys were simply considered orphan wards of the prince.

◆ ◆ ◆

Feelharmonica trusted Ritius, all the more because he was so consistent, insistent, and persistent. Feelharmonica settled back into his sofa.

"But you somehow don't think Koolkup is a problem that needs to be solved."

"I'm just asking questions," Ritius said.

"Either way it needs to be solved."

"Let me tell you a story. You remember your father's policies regarding the northern principality. The expulsions and expropriations? sending thousands of New Gardeners streaming south? where they fire the hearts of the others with their tales of dispossession, to which their scars and missing limbs bear witness? Those nettlesome snakebearers, biting our ankles in the south?"

"Of course. Koolkup has done well with them. He has even reclaimed my uncle's lands near Princeton."

"Yes, he seems to have them and the Illadelphians firmly in hand."

"You say 'Illadelphians' like they are one thing."

"I know better. It is just a manner of speaking. We know what goes on in the south. I want that spoken. I want to talk to you about the north."

"Proceed."

"One of my oldest long ago boys, Balloony Louis, from Eo…He was with us in your father's house for a while, but you probably don't remember him. He moved north after the war, a couple years before Six Bridges. A born businessman, believe, he left his family and his respectable home to make a name for himself in Paramus…to establish an outpost up there for him and his partners, even before the seizures. After the expulsions, he petitioned your father for the right to operate several choice concerns. There was a furniture paint shop finishing goods for New York cabinetmakers, and there was a beer bottler and distributor. The latter was problematic, because a significant portion of the deliveries were to bodegas in Brooklyn. Getting back and forth across the bridge in a manner befitting a profit-making enterprise was impossible, as his trucks were robbed and his drivers were killed.

"He was relieved when your brother Prince Razorbeem took over administration of the northern principality. He expected support of a certain kind, but he did not receive it. Razorbeem finished his father's work there, and since has concerned himself almost exclusively with management of the waters, the dams, and the power supply.

"Water and power are vital infrastructure, given safety and security. But the latter were *not* given, and my boy and his colleagues had been forced to fend for themselves, paying what they must to whom they must for security and safe passage. That, I'm sure you agree, is disgraceful."

Feelharmonica didn't respond.

"So Balloony went to speak with your brother Prince Razorbeem. He is prideful, and he balked at first, but my boy had brought other operators to testify as well, and Razorbeem began to understand that commerce itself is infrastructure, as are business relationships in general. He learned the lesson that you reproach your older brother for learning too well."

Ritius paused to allow the prince to appreciate the symmetry. Feelharmonica gave him nothing and, stonefaced, cocked his head slightly.

"Those two princes, your older and younger brothers, in the absence of any new teaching, have come to learn that they must make their own separate peace with New York, given our historical entanglement."

"My father wanted a new relationship with New York."

"And he might have forged it had he lived. Meanwhile, to your north and to your south you have two separate relations, each a sprawling collage of compromise and convenience, mastered by no common vision."

"Don't think that I am blind to your concerns. I have spoken with both my brothers," Feelharmonica stood and walked behind the sofa. "About this and more than *you* know."

Ritius sat silently.

"Koolkup is preoccupied with the defense of our southern and western borders, it is true. We cannot minimize his efforts on our behalf," Feelharmonica admitted. "But Razorbeem," Feelharmonica paused. "He called me a warlord last time we talked," Feelharmonica chuckled like a cough. "You believe the nerve of that little peasy-headed, stunted growth, platform shoe–wearing poseur? Anyway, when we talk, he reminds me that our kingdom rests upon but a single support and, like you, old friend, he repeats himself, saying that we have no power independent of New York, and that we live like mosquitoes, sucking the blood of those with whom we have nothing else to do. We can hardly increase our sucking power, because even our current position was purchased too dearly."

"Neither of your brothers is a fool. But my story is not done. You and I are sitting here and we have understood and spoken the truth that each prince is forging his own policy with regards to New York. But we know only the one and not the other."

Feelharmonica was surprised at the suddenness with which this new knowledge had taken shape, before his eyes, with his own participation. He was shaken by the sheer size of the hole it revealed in his understanding, struck by the fact that he had already known every fact required to understand, and humbled by how wisely his old friend and counselor had revealed it. He could not speak, but he swallowed and stood, still.

"Your brother Razorbeem took Balloony's concerns to heart. He solicited bids for security services—I believe he met with Councilor Justice Boniface, given that she runs market security here, in New Ark proper. They were unable to come to terms, but your brother made armored vehicles available to certain merchants, and provides armed escort for a modest *per diem*."

"ok, so he is behaving as he should," Feelharmonica noted. "But how can he safely disperse so many men? Smallest lands, smallest numbers."

"My friend answered me well when I asked him the same question. Your brother has his garrison between Paterson and Paramus, near the bend in the Passaic. He requires that merchants report there at the beginning of the week, one week before they require his escort, to preserve their place with a deposit of gold only. So, he was there, waiting in the lobby to see the administrator. The prince and his bodyguard crossed the hall and paused. They were not to be alone, because another group of men was rushing to join them. That second group were workmen of different sorts, tools and implements strapped to their belts like six guns. They exited the building and entered their vehicles outside, and it was a large caravan, with several armored passenger vehicles, more than two pickup trucks, and what struck my friend the most was the large armored tractor with an open trailerbed, on which was installed machinery unlike he had ever seen, and had only ever even heard of. It was some sort of large crane or wench."

"It sounds like he was heading out to inspect the waterways."

"That's what I thought, too."

"Well?"

"That's also what my friend thought."

"So?"

"All the vehicles were marked with the seal of the King of New York."

Feelharmonica froze, trembling, and clutched the back of the sofa to steady himself. When he released it, he pursed his lips and walked back around to sit again with Ritius. Ritius let him gather himself, and sipped from his tumbler while waiting for his prince to speak.

"Now we know the shape of both relations."

"We do, in general. But we do not know the price Razorbeem pays."

"Let's assume that it is too high."

"Yes," Ritius agreed.

"I guess you're waiting for me to ask you for your counsel."

"Yes."

"You think I would shoot the messenger here."

"No," Ritius replied agreeably.

"I need to pull a tooth to get you to say something now? You've already spoken so freely, my friend."

Ritius most definitely did not want to play diplomatic games, but he wanted to hear for himself the prince's first utterances after this new knowledge. He continued.

"I have been your man for years. I have fought for you. I have guarded your life with my own. I have had the honor of serving as one of your counselors. You know me." Ritius set his glass down and leaned forward over the table. "You say that I repeat myself, but I have also repeated my conviction that only you can establish the kingdom your father failed to found. You can. But you are doing nothing to that end while your brothers work toward even others. Even with your privilege as *primo enterprise*, you need a plan and you need your brothers to agree to what you propose. What exactly are you doing?"

Ritius realized that Feelharmonica was waiting for him to finish, and that he was no longer listening. Ritius sat back, rested his hands on his knees, and concluded by trying to state matters as forcefully as he could.

"To me, it looks like you are attacking some of your most beloved citizens, and spending time and money that you cannot afford, in order to drag building materials up the face of Orange Mountain, to build a museum, of all things, to mock a world long dead."

Feelharmonica nodded conservatively, in the manner indicating that one has listened carefully. He took a deep breath and a swallow of his liquor, and a considerate silence filled the parlor.

"Are you feeling sentimental about your brother?" Feelharmonica asked coldly, no expression on his face. Ritius knew that he had upset and alarmed Feelharmonica with his analysis, and that Feelharmonica might be seeking to turn the tables, to make himself feel better by belittling or mocking Ritius. His affectlessness could be convenient cover. It could also be sincere. Ritius chose his words carefully.

"It's not personal. I believe the policy to be misguided."

The prince blinked, and seemed to settle himself. "Do you know about this game they play?"

"I know something about it," Ritius admitted. "I've never seen it played."

"Who chooses the topics presented?"

"No one. The presenter. It's not directed."

"Are the presentations approved?"

"No."

"Is there any review of any kind?"

"No. Well, the group applauds or decries the presentation. The matter is decided there."

"Is this true for both factions?"

Ritius realized that he had only been answering for his brother's side. "Now that you mention it, there are differences between the two factions. The one is as I have described, and the other is different."

"The faction decides as a matter of policy the area of research and presentation, from what I understand," Feelharmonica said.

"Yes, they identify an area ripe for what they call exclusion, and they work for weeks, months, and sometimes years to conclude such a project."

"The whole group undertakes a project?"

"There are teams, I gather."

"Who decides to undertake a project?"

"I am not sure how they decide, but the leader of that faction is one of the original recordkeepers, Tellem Ralph."

"If there are teams, then there is a division of labor, which means there is some decisionmaking process, which means there is a decider."

"I think that must be the case."

"What can be the result of such a project? Do they produce documents? Are their findings presented in 'game' form?"

"The research itself fills rooms, but the result is a relatively small document outlining the result. They compile lists of references and the like."

"But the result is usually some sort of yes or no thing, right? A decision whether this or that could possibly have happened?"

"Exactly right. They comb through libraries, archives, artifacts, documents of any and every sort in order to produce history."

"But it's quite the opposite, isn't it? They eliminate possibilities."

"Yes, that's right."

"Another way to put it is that they remove controversy."

"I suppose one could put it that way," Ritius had to agree. The two men shared a silence. "But the price is a whole mess of martyrs."

"It's all to the glory and power of our kingdom...to be. You can't put a price on that."

Warrior and War

What kind of man enlists and fights in war, and then re-enlists and fights again? What kind of man devotes his life to a prince? Such devotion is an incommutable death sentence with an unknown time and place of execution. This man, this warrior, is different from the kind of man who risks his life in larceny. A warrior may act identically to a bandit, but a warrior requires something that no racket can provide. A warrior requires to kill with honor for meaning. There have been many attempts by various gangs of villains and assorted lowlifes to rationalize their outlawry, and they say too much. Stories told in films, plays and books have sought to understand these creatures, when there is really nothing to understand. The best story was that of "family" among the *mafiosi* of the oldentimes northeastern and middle-western parts of the United States, but that is clearly a lie, because fear destroys the criminal's family first. They can no longer believe that he will provide for their future and they must consider that he will turn out to be a burden and a liability. The crook is a useless person who, for one reason or another, has found no way to achieve a life of meaning. Their actions have no meaning, and the form of their lives is such that meaning is not even approached. They play a deadly game for pathetic stakes, and they must lose. Incarceration is a loss from which there is no recovery, and for which there is no just compensation, because nothing can be done in prison that cannot be done in the world. Death merely confirms what his family feared all along.

The warrior acts in accordance with the strategic vision of the state, as elaborated by the prince he serves. The warrior thereby serves the strength of the state and the authority of the sovereign.

But this gets us no closer to the essential truth of war nor to the essence of the warrior. Neither does the contradiction between the honorable act of the warrior and the disreputable act of the criminal, though they be the same act.

The truth of war is that it is only possible because the warrior exists. The warrior exists because there is a line in the heart of every man that when crossed demands a response. This is the line of ultimate concern, and it triggers ultimate response, as variable as those concerns and responses may be, from man to man. The warrior is the man who can move that line himself, so that his very soul will cry out at matters as abstract as the placement of a vehicle on a bridge, the change of personnel at an embassy, or the look in the eye of a man in a crowd.

This is not the same as the degenerate who kills a man for reckless eyeballing or for scuffing his shoes. That man is not in control even of his own emotions, let alone the subtle mechanisms of the heart and soul that produce them. Moreover, the warrior is one who is comfortable negotiating—and renegotiating—the placement of that line according to his born or bred sense of honor. That balancing act is his spiritual practice. That is his prayer. The warrior may give his entire life and being to his prince, but consider the strength such service requires. What is it? It is the stuff of massacres, unmarked graves, poison gas, smallpox blankets, lynchings, and pogroms. It is also the stuff of mutinies and revolutions.

Warriors can change their minds.

Ex Nihilo and the Exclusion of Possible Pasts

There were no circumstances under which Tellem Ralph, Fila's old friend, would have missed Fila's daughter's naming ceremony.

Rytius was still in the home of Prince Appall back when Tellem, one of Fila's boys from home, was also Fila's friend and helper, sourcing materials, trading records, finding documentation, calling upon those who might have or know more. The first time anyone ever had what would come to be called a listening party, it was at Tellem's Crib, his own record store, then devoted to records in the sciences, technology, and economics, opened after he recovered from injuries sustained during the discovery: he and Fila had taken tube packets of gunpowder and plenty of fuses, but the packets were too large for the door, even with the debris. They blasted a section of concrete off of the I-beam crossing the door and it hit Tellem in the quadriceps, just above the knee tendon. It was a curiously undamaging injury, considering the velocity and mass of the shrapnel, and it was miraculous that he walked on two legs ever again, let alone that he hobbled into the main hall of the library, triumphant, three stories above, three stories below, an authentic oldentime collection of technical and economic knowledge. So now Tellem swung and clacked a black walnut cane with an air of affectation, though he never mentioned his injury.

The issue that long ago evening, October 10, 2133, was a series of periodicals called the *Lancet*, a medical journal, whose series, like that of all the journals Tellem had then recently found, quite inexplicably ceased in 2035. The question Tellem raised was loaded in such a way that friends would understand and forgive his small transgression, because they knew what he meant. Which is to say that his first observation was that this journal, the *Lancet*, published a collection of articles each month, and had for more than a century. A recordkeeper named Cococreem Jennings, a nutritionist at New Ark General, and therefore sensitive to a certain kind of medical development, noted that there was nothing special at all about a journal publishing for a long time. Tellem didn't respond, but continued with his second observation, which was that the collection of articles was usually themed around some medical or scientific issue relevant to their audience. A recordkeeper named Erron asked whether this thematic principle of publication was notable compared to other journals of the time, if Tellem knew that. Tellem answered Erron first a clear no, but not because every single journal he discovered ended the same year, but because, while out of those hundreds of technical, economic, business, and scientific journals he had discovered he had only been able to skim through a couple dozen, every single one was organized according to the same principle: some sort of general theme for the issue which, while not absolutely exclusive of material outside the theme, definitely weighs heavily in the issue. Tellem continued with his third observation, which was that the medical journal at issue had no overriding thematic interest lasting longer than a year or two at any time ever. He paused and asked his loaded question whether that did not immediately rule out any medical or biological cause of the great rip in time that was whatever occurred summer 2035.

Those gathered fell silent and, according to Fila, a recordkeeper named Kloz Munro muttered a profanity to himself, stood up and started clapping, firmly, insistently, and the whole group rose to celebrate Tellem's achievement. His simple question demonstrated the power they sought and the glory they lived for: the power of even a cursory glance at the mere form of the mere history of a single medical journal to clarify historical perspective and thereby create actual substantive historical knowledge. There could have been no worldkilling plague.

But why load that particular question, and not another? What if Tellem had been thinking about something—anything—other than cataclysms in human history? There was clearly nothing to justify plucking pandemic from the universe of possible nonevents… Did the material itself—a stack of magazines—demand this negative, inverted approach? Was there something beyond the magazine-stackness of the material to justify it? Tellem had violated the rules of the game by leaving those questions unanswered. But the results were astonishing.

So Tellem went through his records seeking this sort of knowledge, and he found it. He then asked for help, and those who joined him took the same backward path to knowledge, and they found it. There were no indications of catastrophe along any of the familiar lines one might expect from a basic working knowledge of twenty-first-century history. Tellem's work, the exclusion of possible pasts, remains the indisputable triumph of recordkeeping to date and its only publicly heralded achievement. It was also the limit of what could be achieved with Tellem's formal historical method. And he knew it.

The posse he raised among the recordkeepers threw themselves into their work with the desperate enthusiasm of millenarians rearranging their prophetic calendar. They were determined to isolate via the accumulation of exclusions the cause of the chasm in history. Of course, to fill out any space of unknown mass and extent is a task of unknown work and duration. It can be no surprise when one comes to discover that it takes a *je ne sais quoi*, some *Fingerspitzengefühl*, a couple hints, a little English, some topspin, a push in the right direction—some notion of the shape of the universe one seeks to map.

The gentlest push when investigating unknown domains is *any* hypothesis what will be found. Which is to say, one requires some sort of speculation on what may have happened, and the material may not tell you that it did, but it may tell you that it could not have happened. Via this method, one must invent theoretical events in order to exclude them. One forms a speculation, and goes to disprove it. Of course, the font of speculation is the imagination of the entirely unregulated individual subject, and subject to all the dangers to knowledge that subjectivity entails.

The feverish pace at which they worked, the energy they had, and the regular plodding success of their exclusions spoke for themselves. Their modest slogan was that they were clearing the foundation for the creation of new knowledge. Small successes suffice to fortify those devoted to the life of the mind, and there were those who thought Tellem's strategy was OK, as far as it went, though he was dishonest about its potential to peer across the event horizon, to pull knowledge back out of the rip in time after which they had been fated to live. They disagreed with those who thought Tellem's demagogy, in claiming such ambitions for so crude a method, was reason enough to kick him out and denounce him as a misleader, or even to physically exile him from what was then still called Newark.

There was a single formal inquiry into whether there was any basis for exclusion from recordkeeping, but the truth is that there had been no direct debate over the method of past exclusion, and, the group had not even concluded the previous year's debate over subjectivity in the creation of knowledge, the memory of which was still quite fresh. There were definitely no grounds for exclusion because there were no grounds at all. Tellem's group began calling themselves the Speculative Historians, and the fracture went unset.

Tellem never participated in any public debates on the validity of his method, nor were the fundamentals reopened. He would not debate publicly whether recordkeeping was the same activity as speculative history, though, according to Kloz, he has always insisted, informally, that it is, or at least that "it should be." Which is no answer at all.

◆ ◆ ◆

"The simple truth is that the olden ones had a power too great for their grasp," Tellem continued. The subject of the debate up to that point is unclear.

"Could be, could be… But you haven't gotten around to the issue," Sosoface Ferndale, a private courier from Monmouth, pressed the issue.

"I'm saying, the olden ones could split atoms, and fly around the moon, and manage riven populations as formless masses, pressing the people like clay into the empty places around the market-tested wire-frame axes of their power sculptures. That's taking too much of God's power."

"Yes, God is a jealous God," Sosoface agreed.

"Indeed, and this is at least part of the reason why we don't even know what happened. Consider the implications of the fact that we have this blindness in our history. A wall past which we cannot see, touch, or feel, past which no living memory remains."

"We arise out of a sort of darkness. You state the problem well."

"I'm trying to solve it, if you listen to me. Remember how I phrased the problem to start: the olden ones had a power too great for their grasp. Didn't you show *Frankenstein* recently?"

"No, it was *Rocky Horror Picture Show*," Sosoface answered.

"Well, same difference, in any case, though I myself prefer original sources. Or as close to original as you can get for the thing being investigated, which in this case is popular mentality and understanding of the danger of scientific and technical prowess escaping the control of the creators, and in those days, the people felt that they were among those responsible for such things, though they also felt incapable of rising to the responsibility."

"Alright, go on then."

"I can argue that all social horror, in actuality and in literary and other representation, is a version of the sorcerer's apprentice. It is all about systems going haywire, leaders destroying themselves and their lands on the basis of the very strategy that brought them to power, individuals rationalizing themselves out of their minds, marvels turning monstrous," Tellem threatened rhetorically.

"I can't see what you're doing here, but I'll grant you all of that," Sosoface said.

"So that's all one one hand. One the other hand, let's go back to that wall in history, shading that darkness out of which we emerge. It means something. Just by itself, it means something for what we do. We are people of culture and learning, and we live for the joy of placing ourselves in the flow of history. We feel ourselves…, no, we know ourselves to be the only ones capable of rising to the responsibility of recovery, recognition, and hopefully one day restoration of the best of the past. But God has made it so that we cannot possibly have it. We cannot ever establish real continuity. This is a message in itself."

"I know one thing: we all want to know what you think it means," Sosoface said, tiring of Tellem's rhetoric.

"I got some ideas about what he thinks it means," said D-Man, teasing Tellem.

"Yeah, me too," sighed Sosoface.

"Listen, you all want to act like you don't see this elephantine impediment to understanding in your face, you so-called recordkeepers. You seek to know the past through its artifacts, and you should know this best of all. This is the problem with your method, which is hardly a method at all."

"Still ain't answered the question," announced Sosoface.

"Got to the point neither," said D-Man.

"It's going to sound crazy coming from me," Tellem warned those listening, for he and Sosoface had gathered an audience, "but you can't penetrate this mystery with data. You can't get the proper perspective collecting these messages in bottles."

"Regardless of the epistemological difficulties involved, in principle there is nothing preventing historical speculation on artifacts. We do it all the time," said Sosoface, glad finally to have a target.

"That's what's in all the notes," agreed D-Man.

"Exactly. And we put all the arguments in commentaries and record all the sources in appendices and you know how all this goes and how we build on each other's work," concluded Sosoface.

"But you won't ever be open to the deepest meanings of what you find," Tellem said.

"You just want to jam your prophecies into the fragments you find. And you don't want to take the time to arrange those fragments, to actually tease out the relationships they themselves declare," Sosoface said, just laying it all out. He did not expect Tellem to argue forthrightly or even coherently, but he knew from exactly which perspective, frame of reference, and point of view Tellem was coming.

"Let the man finish," Fila said, coming up behind GJ.

"Thank you, brother," said Tellem.

"More than brothers. Friends," Fila smiled warmly.

"That's the truth, Ruth," Tellem's smile waned and he held Fila's gaze for a moment. "I think you might like to hear this, too, boo, 'cause as I was saying, I think I may, I think I might, have found a vein of bright pyrite." Tellem rubbed his hands together, pantomiming greedy glee. Olden slang for pyrite was "fool's gold" because of its appearance (ignoring the fact that it can indicate real gold nearby), so among the Speculative Historians, pyrite became slang for a new source of speculations, a new field in which to begin reaping pasts.

"Oh, yeah?" Fila asked. "How long have you been working on it?"

"'Bout five, six months," responded Tellem.

It wasn't that a silence fell, but that those gathered loosened their grip on their own conversations, and began to let silences linger so that they could overhear.

"I haven't heard anything about it," Fila said, surprised there had been no gossip, controversy, or bragging about a half-year project, presumably involving new artifacts and documents.

"Well, you wouldn't. This one's special," Tellem winked. "But I phrase things a certain way for a reason," he continued, dramatically. Tellem was enjoying himself again. "My man Fila knows what I mean. Us old-school fellows, right? Anyway, the reason I put the danger the way I did, is because I believe the olden ones really did do it to themselves and ourselves, in a way they weren't expecting. In fact, in a way that just smacked them clean upside the head. There's only one possible past that explains both the wall, the darkness, and the cool placidity of olden-days technical and economic discourse approaching 2035. If you take to heart the inductive-plausibility principle that underlies all our activity, the ethic by which we must always account for the most significant of the most of the thing… well, if you believe that, as I do… I say that the arrival of general artificial intelligence is the only event capable both of causing the collapse and cleaning so thoroughly up after itself, imposing silence where there was surely noise—weeping, wailing and gnashing of teeth."

"That's what you want to exclude now?" asked Sosoface.

"I believe that this is actually the thing that created the gap in our history," Tellem said.

"But it doesn't matter if it's GAI or not," said Sosoface.

"You're going to have to explain that one, son," chuckled Tellem.

"You simply won't understand that this is not about saving us from catastrophe or recovering the past. The apocalypse already happened. This is about building the future," Sosoface maintained.

"Out of what?" Tellem asked.

"Out of the past, of course," Sosoface said.

"So, whats the problem with having an answer to the question?"

"If this is the answer, and let's stipulate that it is, so what?"

"I think you don't understand how important this is."

"Why? Why is it important? I just asked you. It's true. AI destroyed the world. So what?"

"Do you know how long we've been seeking the answer to this question?"

"Since sometime around the end of the North Atlantic Wars."

"That's right, but it's not right, and you know damned well what I'm talking about. This ain't no little piece of poetic literary cultural trivia. This is important."

"I've asked you why twice. Make this three times."

"How can we move into the future if we don't know the past?"

"Because we'll make the same mistakes and all that?" Sosoface asked.

"Exactly."

"The answer is to think even through platitudes and not to believe that we understand something because it sounds familiar. We can't possibly make the same mistakes, or even the same kind of mistake, because the world is entirely different. If you propose that we might be in danger of making mistakes that are somehow similar to those of the past we'd have to have a discussion about what similarity means, and I know you don't like stuff like that," Sosoface said.

Floweria said "Oops," and somebody giggled.

"And even if we do need cautionary tales, we can discover them by treating the records with proper respect, discovering what they mean, instead approaching them arrogantly seeking to find."

"Very nice. Remember, I've been at this just as long as you." Tellem had been at the work much longer than Sosoface, and this was one of the frustrations of arguing with Tellem. Sometimes he was unexpectedly generous, and this surprised opponents who expected bad faith at all times. It also made his opponents waste energy trying to scope out his angle. He had an unethical mode of presentation, in which he relied upon commonplace constructions and well-worn associations, while never quite constructing or making them himself.

"I know," Sosoface admitted cheerfully.

"We've excluded hundreds of pasts. What have you done?" Tellem took it to the mat. This, of course, was not a genuine challenge, but an attempt to close discussion and save face.

Fila could no longer allow Tellem to slide. To have dared to raise, or even to seem to circle around fundamental issues, on a day like today, after having avoided it for literal years and years, was a bridge too far.

"Wait a minute," Fila said. "I don't think…that's not what our work is about."

"I know it, but listen. Now we're at a point where, among the pasts that present themselves, we *may* have scraped all away that are false. All that remains can only be true."

"You're switching stuff up again, talking about truth. You and Sosoface weren't talking about truth, but an answer to a question. Answering that one question is the basis of your entire project."

"True," Tellem drawled slowly, laughing, redirecting Fila's accusation. But he was eager to get back on his favored terrain, and he was hopeful that Fila would ease them back into their corners. "But it's a fundamental question."

"Maybe it is, maybe it's not," Fila said. "Sosoface is right. You can't really say why the answer is important, or even why the question is important. You've been sliding back and forth between them so much that you've gotten them confused."

"Yeah, my bad," Tellem retreated. "Honestly, if you see these gray whiskers in my beard you might imagine that I know better than to argue with fools. You'd be wrong." He put himself up for martyrdom, tireless dogged plodding on behalf of the good and the true. He just cared too much to give up on his comrades whose minds had been hurt in battle with darkness. But he was on the verge of capitulation: "If you don't see why uncovering the mystery is important, I don't know what to tell you," Tellem shrugged and waved his arms in exasperation, and looked around to commiserate with those looking and listening.

"Our comrade here has asked you four times what changes if this mystery is answered that way. I know what you want, Tellem. See, I know you," Fila said, louder, standing now. He would not allow Tellem to approach, muddy, and then run away from issues he had been avoiding since the very beginning. Not today. "You want to find, after a year or two of frenzied activity that, no, AI could not have been the cause after all. Free to cast your nets again, you'll keep searching, speculating.

There's always something to drag up. Meanwhile, over the years, you have avoided all discussion of our aims, goals, strategies, tactics, to just plow through thousands of artifacts and volumes, sometimes more than once, blind the whole time to what you're actually looking at."

"Well, good evening, folks," Tellem smiled and turned theatrically to take his leave. "I think it might be time to go get me a good seat and a hot plate instead of this here hot seat in a bad place," he said, chuckling amiably. Folks opened a space to let him pass.

"Don't leave now. Listen, you have accomplished a lot. We know it," Fila wanted to make himself clear. Tellem did stop and turn to listen. Fila continued.

"But you have to know that to us, it's not clear what your work really means. I think you have to admit that you don't even really know exactly what your work means, if it doesn't result in a miraculous mystery solution that bowls everyone over with its clarity and necessity. You have come to expect this, to rely on this future revelation, and you believe it will justify your difficulties plodding, and, yes, of course, explain the suffering and enslavement of mankind. Yes, you are definitely creating knowledge, but your methods are ultimately superficial and inappropriate," Fila continued.

"You take record collections—sometimes *the whole* record collection—and, using your wits and what you have learned to date, you bind them together in theory, by posing a property that you believe to hold across the collection. If the past was A, then property x must hold. If the speculation is properly formed, any case in which x does not hold means that past A did not occur. You have made progress, by construction, mathematically. Excluding any one of infinite possible pasts must be counted as progress. The problem is that your method has no way of recognizing the historical necessity of any possible past it *fails to exclude*. You all have gone through every record we have at least once and still haven't developed a sense of history, because you ignore the relationships the materials themselves embody and express. If GAI was the apocalypse, how would you actually know? You would just keep searching to exclude it forever. Your work can never end, because you'll never know when you're done," Fila concluded. "You do busy work."

Tellem had already bragged about how many exclusions the Speculative Historians had made, and decided that it would sound peevish and weak were he to repeat it. He said nothing.

"But it is true that you perform miracles, and I'm glad you brought that up. To pull substance from form is one of the ways in which man is like God, remember? It's not like anything else, and it's as seductive and dangerous as anything after which man has lusted. Erron's here today… You remember his commentaries on the Bible, cross-referenced with his concordance of pre-Lutheran Christian doctrine. God created the world in six days, resting on the seventh because His work was complete. The substance was accomplished. He did not do anything else until He rescued the Hebrews from Egypt, resting again until He sent His son into Rome, where He offered to redeem humanity of sin, and preached that all people are children of God. The substance in that case was an idea. That idea is the basis of all doctrines of equality, liberty, and justice that man has had the nerve to speak. The substance was accomplished, and it is appropriate that God has done nothing since. He leaves to us the desperate compulsion to act when there is nothing to do. Erron calls it the power of mess making. It requires hubris, so it can only be human. But given that it is a perversion of λόγος, as though one were addicted to creation, it is only quasi divine."

Assembly

Carnation had Rytius at a table with Floweria Giddens, the baker, and D-Man Furness, the blacksmith, a married couple of recordkeepers with deep roots in Eo, on both their families' sides. Hunnybunny Henry, a language arts teacher and modern dancer, and her boyfriend Wascal Chase, STEM teacher, were Speculative Historians, but that's only because her parents had been social-science teachers who knew Tellem personally. They came to most of the games anyway, and had presented more than a few of their own. And then there was the lovely Vinilla Breem and her 11-year-old daughter Light. Light was the youngest ever to play the game, and her first presentation had been on cartoon tricksters, and particularly the relationship between Anansi and Bugs Bunny. Rytius still hadn't told anyone about the letter to his brother or the prince and the Tower of Records. It was past breakfast and before lunch but, aside from the whiskey, he had so far only slurped at a smoothie—a calming potion with carrot, celery, pineapple, cucumber, beet, and kale—putting off bringing it up, and he ran a dumb hydraulics quasi experiment whereby he measured how long it took the fluid to rise to the top of the straw as all the ice, pulverized into smoothie grain fluid dust, defrosted and turned back to water. Almost everybody in the hall was finished eating, and just sort of picking at bones and licking spoons clean.

"Y'all heard about Huggums?" Wascal asked Floweria, D-Man, Rytius, and Vinilla.

"No…?" Floweria answered. "Do tell."

Rytius didn't say anything, and Hunnybunny interrupted anyway. "I don't want to hear all that again right now, Wascal," she said. "Let's have a good time celebrating today."

"You're right," Wascal replied. "How's the food Rytius?" he asked, gesturing at his uneaten plate of grits, mussels, and dandelion greens.

"Yeah. You're not going to eat anything?" Vinilla asked him, smiling.

"I'm not hungry yet," Rytius answered.

"How can you grow up to be big and strong if you don't eat anything?" her daughter Light asked him.

He laughed. "But I'm already grown up!"

"You sure?" asked Wascal, smirking.

"No, not really," chuckled Rytius.

"He fills up on duck eggs daily before leaving the house," Floweria playfully defended him.

"Goose eggs, you mean," D-Man said. "He sells all the duck eggs."

"Well, not all of them," Rytius said.

"You know how to cook, Rytius?" Vinilla asked him.

"I can burn a couple of things," he said, smiling. "Name something and I bet I can make it."

"Hmm," Vinilla pondered the challenge. "I wonder." She was trying to come up with something challenging but not outrageous. Like lasagna.

"You cook all your own food?" asked Wascal.

"Yeah, mostly," Rytius said.

"There's some things that don't taste right unless you make them yourself," Floweria said.

"Yeah, but that's usually only 'cause that's how your mother used to make it," D-Man said, refining the point.

"And if it's not *exactly* how you want it, you can't eat it," Hunnybunny added.

"It's the narcissism of small differences, and the tiniest is all it takes," Floweria said. "Like sweet pickles instead of dill pickles in potato salad."

"Ew!" squealed Hunnybunny. "Gross."

"That's what I'm saying," D-Man vehemently agreed.

"You never eat at the restaurants or sandwich stands or anything like that?" Wascal asked Rytius. "There's a gang of them over where you stay at."

"Not really," he answered.

"It can get expensive," Vinilla offered, wondering whether Rytius might be a bit too frugal.

"No, it's not that," he responded, smiling. The speed of his denial struck him. He did not want Vinilla to think he was a cheapskate. But she must have known that he was from a powerful family, and that money probably wouldn't ever really be a problem for him. "It's just flavor and quality."

"Ooh, an Epicurean," Hunnybunny teased.

"You like crispy crawlers?" Wascal asked.

"Sure," Rytius answered, trying to remember where he put his rooping iron.

"Oh. I just thought you might be a vegan or something," Wascal continued, looking at Rytius's smoothie.

"No, I eat meat," he answered. "How else could I have grown up so big and strong?" He grinned at Light, flexed his biceps, and laughed.

Light appreciated that, and Rytius realized that he had also most likely been flexing his muscles for Vinilla, which made him feel silly and juvenile.

"Are you a vegan? Or vegetarian?" Rytius asked Wascal.

"No, I eat everything. Almost everything. I stopped eating out, though," Wascal said.

Floweria raised an eyebrow and cocked her head at Hunnybunny, who swallowed a chuckle. D-Man smirked, and Vinilla tried her best to ignore it for the sake of her daughter.

"I think you've got the right idea, though," Wascal proceeded, not acknowledging his double entendre. "You can't go wrong cooking for yourself."

"Indeed," Rytius agreed. "And you can save money, too. Ahem." He shot a smile and a glance at Vinilla.

"I would keep it up if I were you," Wascal noted.

"And you can impress any ladyfriends you might have a mind to entertain," D-Man came with an assist.

"Oh, well, in that case, I would like grilled chicken salad this evening," Floweria said sweetly, leaning over and fluttering her eyelashes at D-Man.

"Look at you, Rytius, got me running my mouth, getting myself in trouble," he said, turning to kiss Floweria. Rytius would have blushed if he could have.

"It's no trouble at all. Not if you make some artichokes, too," Floweria continued, presenting her face for another kiss from D-Man. He obliged. "With that chili-ginger dipping sauce I like."

"Don't forget dessert, girl," noted Hunnybunny.

"We'll talk about that later," Floweria said.

Rytius couldn't continue his light flirtation with Vinilla after such a public display of affection, so he decided the time had finally come to change the subject and share his new knowledge.

"I have some news," he said to his tablemates.

"Oh, yeah?" D-Man asked. Rytius realized he was speaking too softly, and that he needed to address the entire dining hall.

"I HAVE SOME NEWS I NEED TO SHARE WITH YOU ALL," Rytius barked, standing. No one didn't fall silent and turn to listen. "First I want to say how much I appreciate Fila and his family and I want to say something about how I feel the truth of what he was saying before, before his beautiful daughter Firebrite chose her name." He swallowed hard and continued. "My brother—you all know my brother, Ritius, one of Prince Feelharmonica's men. I received a letter meant for him from the prince this morning, and I read it by mistake, thinking it was for me. It had some instructions for my brother, regarding a tower Feelharmonica is building. The prince is building this tower atop Orange Mountain, and he means it to be a tower of records. He instructed my brother to collect our records to fill it."

He ceased speaking and observed his colleagues's faces. They expected additional words clarifying the nonsensical message he had just delivered. He remained silent, swallowed, and focused on his breathing while calmly looking from face to face, meeting eye to eye. Sugarpic was the first to understand, and he knew that because her face cracked and she desperately searched his face for any sign of anything further. Her husband GJ croaked loudly involuntarily something like "Aw," or "Naw," and left his mouth open like that. Rytius sought out Fila among those seated and saw him, met his eyes, and Fila betrayed no emotion at all. Surely his mind was spinning, as was Rytius's own that morning. Perhaps he did not believe the news either. Tellem was the first to break the silence.

"Why?" he asked, loud but plaintive. This set off an uproar, and there was rattling of utensils and slamming of fists and furious damnations all around.

Rytius attempted to answer over the din. "Ritius…Look, Ritius…" Folks fell silent to let him finish. "Ritius didn't tell me why." Those gathered felt that Rytius deserved further recrimination, and they gave it to him loud. Rytius tried to continue, and he yelled that Ritius probably didn't know why himself, but somebody screamed and a green bean hit him in the middle of his forehead and slid down his nose. He wiped his face and opened his mouth to speak, but Carnation was suddenly in his face, and he thought she might be trying to comfort him, but she was yelling for people to stop throwing stuff and Vinilla was removing several other green beans from his headdress. He closed his mouth while Carnation shielded him and Vinilla cleaned him, while those gathered got the initial shock out of their system. The green beans had been simmered in a tangerine butter sauce, which was quite good.

BB bumped his belly against a long bench table before him when he stood, and it moved, loudly scraping the floor of the dining hall, which is no easy feat, considering that such bench tables typically seat 12 comfortably. The unmistakable screech of the scrape commanded such attention that he hardly had to hold his hands up and gently pat the air to calm the ruckus before asking gently, "Why didn't you ask?" Folks started getting mad again, so BB held one hand aloft, and delivered Rytius the malicious accusation nearly all felt he deserved thus far: "And *are you going to?*"

"Of course I am going to ask him. He's coming by my record store tomorrow morning, to take an inventory. I plan to ask him all about everything we discuss and decide here today," Rytius reminded everyone of their power in the situation, and the muttering faded.

"It was only the circumstances of the letter that made it hard for me to get into all of the questions. But my first question, which I did ask, was what is this tower all about," Rytius continued.

"It could probably be about preserving everything in a nice safe place," said Hunnybunny.

"Yeah, it could be something like a library," said Voom.

"Or maybe a museum," said Rytius, nodding along to encourage the new sense of cooperative discussion emerging from the initial anger and dismay.

"Or a prison," said Fila, souring the mood immediately.

"We don't know anything," said Rytius.

"It's kind of arbitrary, isn't it?" asked Fila.

"Of course it is. All I'm saying is that we need to talk about it."

"In deals like this, the substance of which is entirely one-sided, there's usually something like money changing hands as well," Fila continued. "Please tell me Ritius said something about some kind of money or some kind of consideration or compensation at least."

And with that, Rytius was convicted once more. Someone hissed. He knew that his answer would not elicit mercy. Rytius said "He didn't," and a woman cursed loudly while a large piece of home-fried potato crusted with sauteed garlic, parsley and marjoram flew past his ear. "WAIT A MINUTE, GOD DAMN IT!" he barked, and he turned around threateningly in the direction from which the fry had flown. He felt a glop of something near the back of his headdress, where his hair came out beneath, and so, reluctantly, drawing far too many giggles, he lifted his right hand slowly to the back of his neck to discover the food with which he had been pelted this time. It was a gooey clumpy farina lump. It could have been worse.

"Control," Sugarpie offered.

"Well, yeah," said Fila. "That's obvious."

"I agree, it has to be about control in general, but in particular, I think we can deduce the reason for the confiscation," Kloz began, attempting to be helpful. "The prince cannot stop us recordkeeping or speculating on historical events," he stated diplomatically. "But the prince can stop us working on the materials we have gathered to date. That's the only possible reason for the action."

Rytius was about to respond, but Floweria answered Kloz sharply, quickly, "The action taken is not necessarily bound by date. Perhaps the confiscation is to be ongoing? Perhaps we are to be conscripted to staff a new research library? Perhaps that library is a mere vanity project. Perhaps it is serious. Perhaps the records will be burned because the prince worships ignorance in his every habit and posture? Perhaps the prince just randomly this moment decided to express his hatred for us in policy? To ascribe significance to the current moment on the basis of our knowledge so far is an overstep, I'm sure you recognize."

"Now is not the time to mistake hopes for facts. Is and ought and all of that," Tellem interjected, defending his colleague from the argument threatening close at hand.

"That's right," agreed Rytius.

"We need some sort of plan," Dancy stated the obvious. "I mean if the tower is like a library or museum, do we *want* to be staff? If it's something more like a prison, do we want privileged access or do we simply refuse to cooperate in that case?"

"But what would it mean to refuse to cooperate?" Cococreem asked.

"Do you mean refusal like just saying no or do you mean some sort of self-defense?" Tweety asked Dancy.

"Armed self-defense?" asked Fila.

"Is there any other kind?" BB replied.

"Words in both cases," Wascal proposed.

"Yeah, well, we should think about the worst case," said Voom.

"I haven't worked all that out yet, but let's just say words right now," Dancy answered.

"We're nowhere near the point of discussing battle plans," Rytius interjected. "We don't know near enough yet."

"We know more than enough," Carnation said, sitting back down next to Fila, who stood.

"We can do two things at once. Why don't we start planning our defense," Fila said, drawing approval, "and we also get our questions together now."

"I think that's a bad idea, because it's starting in bad faith," Rytius said. "You know actions and thereby the effects caused by those actions can be clouded by impure intention, bewildering the mind of the actor when their action fails to produce the clarity they expected."

Rytius had known what needed to be said, and he had just been waiting for the right moment to say it. He knew these people, devoted to knowledge and reason in and for a real life well-lived, self-appointed guardians of the spiritual narrows, that sliding space between the concept and the execution, the intellect and the administration, the council and the plan. Reminded of their vocation, they could no longer so easily turn their fear, anxiety, and helplessness to blame Rytius for failing to defend the community singlehanded, by surprise. A more reflective mood descended, sadly.

Tellem stood, scraping his chair. "I think Rytius is right, for what it's worth," he said. "No use going off half-cocked without the proper perspective, frame of reference, and point of view. I'm talking about information, little bits of immediately useful data, like facts, about the concrete situation with this so-called Tower of Records. Facts is what we lacks. But we can get them, and we're going to get them, because this man lives up to his name. I think we need to show our brother here some appreciation for the risks he has taken, and for all he does," Tellem praised Rytius and initiated a round of sustained applause. The record-keepers and the Speculative Historians were ready first to understand their situation, and they were determined then to take whatever actions would be required to continue their work.

Disvotion

Tuesday, February 5, 2143

At the request of his old friend, Balloony arranged for Ritius to meet Prince Razorbeem atop Orange Mountain Tuesday dawn, at the ruins of the old academy, quite close to Feelharmonica's construction site, and not far at all from Little Falls dam, which Razorbeem in any case required to inspect. Ritius had two aims: to discover the price of New York's assistance with his waterways, and to understand the reason for Razorbeem's deception and subterfuge concealing those questionable arrangements—his strategic objective.

He drove himself.

◆ ◆ ◆

One black-windowed black armored truck bearing the white-on-navy betentacled Jolly Roger insignia of the King of New York was parked in front of the bronze eagle sculpture, which once welcomed students. The campus was mostly destroyed, but sections of administration buildings remained, as did a complicated maze, a puzzle really, of concrete and steel retaining walls shaped precisely to purposes now unknown, but which forensic architects might one day study and solve.

Ritius rolled past the truck, reversed, and turned his truck to face the other, leaving a good car-length space between the two. He checked his six guns and thought about removing his shotgun from its sling. He did not, but he exited the vehicle deliberately, never taking his eye off the truck before him. He looked for the slightest shake or tremble in its wheelbase as he exited, because if Razorbeem meant him harm, he would surely strike just as Ritius exited, while he was in other motion.

There was no incident of any kind, because the truck was empty. Ritius first held a silent hand up to hail the driver or other occupant, then he spoke a greeting, and then he barked to call them out. He approached the truck against his animal instinct, though in accord with his better judgment, which was coming to understand that things were not as he expected. He had been and remained appropriately alert to danger, but he was also genuinely scared, because his warning systems were in conflict, and he knew that that was precisely the sort of situation in which fatal mistakes are made: in the seconds it takes to realign instinct with judgment, one could easily fail to recognize the place to which the danger had now moved in the new arrangement of circumstances.

"Ritius," a voice called from behind him. He turned faster than he could ever remember, and he heard the tone indicating that the speaker was not a threat, and did not mean to cause surprise, and he was again disoriented. He stayed his hand from his guns, and wondered whether that was the right thing to do and he had not decided whether it was by the time he actually met Razorbeem's eyes, and knew that Razorbeem was not a threat. He did not feel good about any of this. "Faithful servant of my brother, Prince Feelharmonica."

"You know who I am, and I know you as well. Your brother loves you and appreciates your efforts toward the glower of the kingdom."

Razorbeem smiled softly, and breathed deeply. "My brother may believe this to be a kingdom."

Ritius pricked up his ears and listened.

"By which he means *his* kingdom, I suppose," Razorbeem chuckled and seemed to relax, though he hadn't seemed tense. " 'Daddy made me *primo enterprise*,' " Razorbeem mocked his brother with a simpering whine. "Listen, I don't know how well you study statecraft, so you may or may not understand me, but this is not a kingdom. Perhaps my father could have founded a kingdom here."

"We'll never know." While on one level, his interaction with Razorbeem was already quite a success, Ritius realized that his warning systems were again crossed. He was calmly speaking with the prince of the northern part of North New Jersey, and he was pleasantly surprised to hear his own ideas spoken back to him, but he was still uneasy, and he thought he was uneasy because Razorbeem was entirely too forthcoming, plainly disrespecting his brother Feelharmonica in Ritius's face. Such insults not only reflect badly upon the warrior, because disrespect of one's master is disrespect to one for having chosen such an unworthy master, but they are also direct affronts in themselves, because they are evidence that the speaker holds whatever actions one might take to defend one's master to be of no account at all. Not even worthy of the slightest dissimulation. Perhaps because the speaker has already decided to do away with the warrior.

"You mock my man, the Prince of New Ark. You know how we live," Ritius warned Razorbeem precisely, and not merely formally, even through his anxiety and confusion, which remained.

Ritius had not clarified to himself the precise source of his anxiety, given that it was not only the open mockery of Feelharmonica, because it remained after Ritius clearly addressed it, and he still had not figured it out by the time he noticed to himself that they were still alone, standing in front of the bronze eagle. His unease was washed away in a flood of fresh fear sufficient to stop him breathing and to get him expecting a bullet. The bullet did not come in that second or the next, but he had already spoken and it was Razorbeem's turn again, and he could not under any circumstance convey panic by, for instance, looking around frantically for signs of danger, but he was in such a state that he had to do something immediately to address his security situation.

Razorbeem smiled pleasantly and looked around, breathing deeply of the hilltop air, like a pleasure traveler. "But he is no longer your man, though, is he," Razorbeem stated, as though it were not a question at all.

And with that strategic embrace, Ritius was no longer afraid for his life, but he was entirely disoriented. He tried to put that aside to deal with the matter immediately at hand. "Where is your bodyguard?" he asked Razorbeem, who was proving himself to be a clever and perhaps wise leader of men.

Without hesitation or artifice Razorbeem answered him "Two in trees and one in the ruins over there." Razorbeem waved a hand toward the tumbling columns, several dozen yards away.

"Rifles?" Ritius asked.

"With these special laser sights. Have you used them?"

"I have never used one, though I have seen them used."

"Yeah, the target can't see…Only the shooter. You need these special goggles."

"OK, OK," Ritius relaxed and smiled a small smile of his own, because he could not imagine another scenario here in which he could be surprised or disoriented again. Of course, that was also the problem. His smile vanished in just as relaxed a fashion as it had appeared.

"Shall we walk? I want to see the tower site," Razorbeem suggested.

"I'm just about sick of this eagle, anyway," Ritius said, knocking the sculpture on its beak as they passed. "I wonder why it still stands." Feelharmonica would surely want to destroy any symbol of olden United States patriotism.

"It's a hawk," Razorbeem corrected him, turning and starting off down the footworn wooded path toward the east. "Back in the olden days, the university 'mascot' was a red man who had the power to turn into a hawk."

"Was this known at the time or is this new speculative knowledge?"

"The record of images shows his metamorphosis. And the redskins of old were a glowerful people steeped in the magic of their ancient folk-ways," Razorbeem stopped to inspect the large tree limb blocking their path, and, deciding that it was too large to move, but too small to walk around, he threw one leg over it. Mid-straddle, he continued. "They had names like Red Hawk and Laughing Bear, which seems to indicate that they themselves knew and celebrated their powers of transformation."

Razorbeem threw his other leg over and had to hop down to the ground. He was perhaps a head shorter than Ritius, a little smaller than his brother, who stood up to the lobes of Ritius's ears.

"Watch your leg there…   But don't forget the snakebearers have ancestors as well, and they feared and never ceased their pursuit of these red men, seeking either to subdue them and steal their magic, or have done with them entirely. The story I have heard, and that I believe, is that Red Hawk was kidnapped in one of many pirate raids the snakebearers visited upon the redskins, always with the excuse that it was revenge for another kidnapping, usually of a young virgin girl. The masters of the academy tortured him to reveal his secrets, and he never told. They failed to replicate his magic, and so they kept him imprisoned, bringing him into the sun only when they needed his magic before sporting events and other ceremonies. But as boys will do, he grew into a man, claiming his full power, and so he made the change and flew away home."

Ritius climbed over and they continued down the path toward the construction site. They were not far from the clearing near the top of the mountain, over which one could look and see a large portion of northern New Jersey: Paterson off in the distance, the Manhattan skyline beyond them, Eo just south, New Ark a little past that. Feelharmonica's workers had razed the entire area, and were leveling the ground up so that the tower would be the undisputed king of the mountain. Mounds of earth were pushed back against the wood, and they approached these mounds from behind. They could now feel the rumble of the earthmovers beneath their feet. "The snakebearers would have preferred to ignore the whole thing, but Red Hawk was loved and, moreover, missed. To quell the discontent, the masters of the academy were forced to acknowledge what had happened, and they let the truth be told, changing all images of him to reveal his new form. The people demanded that he also be honored, and that is the meaning of the statue you misunderstand and therefore fail to appreciate."

Ritius nodded and said nothing as they stepped out into the clearing.

"There's not a single orange on this mountain," Razorbeem said, gravely. Then he laughed. "This whole place used to be a volcano, you know. I mean New Ark."

"I had no idea," Ritius said, honestly.

"Before people. This area is a big bowl, and it was flooded with lava three times. But with a gap between, so that there's layers. Just regular dirt and ordinary sediment between the layers of lava rock."

"Like a cake and icing."

"That's right. But then the earth started moving around, making mountains, and some of those layers folded over onto one another, and some just turned over and were driven into the ground."

"You can't really fold a cake," continued Ritius, trying to think of something to compare it to.

"True. Maybe it's like biscuits or apple turnovers. But the other part—the part that got driven underground—it's like a slice of cake on its side. And the rain washed the icing away. These ridges, these mountains here, are the pieces of cake left."

Ritius was impressed with Razorbeem's geological knowledge.

"Lava rock isn't the strongest material. It can withstand a bit of rain," Razorbeem went on. "But if you look across the Bay," he pointed toward Bergen Neck, and the Bayonne ruins. "The granite starts right there. If New York were a cake, the icing between the layers is schist, a sort of heated and compressed shale, which is already harder than the mud and basalt of the New Ark basin. The cake itself, though, the layers, are made of much stronger stuff—marble, granite, and gneiss."

"I suppose that's how it bears such tall buildings."

"It stands to reason."

Reason

There is always a place for reason but it is not very large. In fact, it is cramped and uncomfortable.

Reason has allies only when it does not need them, or when they are throwing it a surprise party, having already vanquished its foes. If reason confronts its enemies alone, it has already lost.

So Rytius, awakened by the sound of hail pellets against the window, began his day wondering again how to deal with his brother. Rytius believed that even if his brother were strictly business, Ritius would readily answer any questions Rytius had, and he had plenty. Like, for instance, what did the prince think he was doing with this tower? He reminded himself not to forget the bit about cash compensation. It would be useful to know what the prince thought about recordkeeping in general. Would the tower be like a large record store, in which listeners and readers could gather, discuss, borrow materials, deposit materials, help with indexing and collation? Floweria had asked who would staff the tower. Would there be fees or restrictions? Would it be open to the public? Would contributing recordkeepers retain special privileges or rights of access? What about sensitive materials? What about protection from theft? What about storage? Rytius had not heard from anyone about the prince reaching out for advice on how to store books, magazines, tapes, films… Heat and humidity require caution even where mere trash is concerned, let alone the concrete artifacts of the history of human thought and expression.

Rytius was turning these questions over in his mind and still had not decided how to put them by the time he heard a truck outside, as closely as anyone could expect to 9 AM. From the side window of the kitchen, Rytius saw his brother approach the door, stop and then turn his head to look directly at him. He smiled, and so did Rytius, lowering his rifle.

◆ ◆ ◆

"So is there some procedure we should follow here?"

"Nothing special. I don't need to get every single title today, just see what you have, generally," Ritius answered easily, smiling gently, as though to communicate his willingness to communicate.

Rytius's normal suspicion where his brother was concerned was surpassed here, and he felt anger rising in his breast, because Ritius had enough sense to know that anyone spending hours and days and years of their lives sifting for no pay through the debris of the world gone by would have everything tabulated, dated, related, and, where possible, replicated. Rytius's anger was coupled with a confusion as to what purpose Ritius would expect such a pretense to serve. Perhaps Ritius was trying to catch Rytius retaining or withholding items of special interest. And that would be an insult, because Ritius also knew that Rytius would be loath to hide his rebellion were he so inclined. These things are matters of honor, and both had taken the same lessons, together.

So rather than continue trying to figure his brother's angle, he decided to obliterate the issue with weapon he had at hand. He handed his brother an accordion folder and considered whether he should kick his brother out after handing it over. "Here's the full, up-to-date inventory."

"The map is not the territory," Ritius said, as he took it. His gentle smile slipped away and his face took on the look of a man with regrets. Rytius's confusion deepened, and he wondered whether he had misunderstood, and decided that it didn't matter because his anger remained.

"You know what I mean. And I taught you that anyway," Rytius said sharply, turning away. He weighed his obligations to his colleagues and himself against his unwillingness to be degraded or insulted and accepted that there was nothing else he could do.

"That's what I'm saying," Ritius smiled again. "But, you know, I just wanted you to take me through." Rytius heard the change in the tone of his brother's voice, and he turned to look again. The look in his brother's eyes, as though he were simultaneously requesting an embrace and apologizing for any misunderstanding and hopeful of a new start and hurt at this small administrative matter between them today, made him feel as though he had not seen his brother in years.

"Oh," Rytius said, now realizing that there was indeed an ulterior motive to his brother's ease of instruction, though it was neither degrading nor a snare, and that he had therefore been unjust to his brother in this particular matter. He did not speak but listened. As he prepared to accept his shame to himself, he wondered sadly whether and how his brother would turn this into some new manipulation.

"I haven't been here in a long time, and I want to see how you're…taking care of the…of our house."

"Uh oh," Rytius chuckled. "Yeah, I didn't patch the roof before the snows this past fall."

"Yeah, but you know what I mean. Listen, I know you spend a lot of time doing this work, and I know how important it is to you. I just want to see what you've been doing. What you're proud of."

If there was one thing Rytius knew, it was not to underestimate his brother, nor to let his guard down on anything not entirely within his own exclusive control. He could not allow his shame at having misunderstood what his brother claimed to be a legitimate interest in his life and work to distort his judgment. He decided to allow his brother freedom in this small range, granting him the benefit of the small doubt that he was not crafting another manipulation. Which made it more important that Rytius be clear about what was and was not under his own exclusive control. He reminded himself that Ritius worked for the prince. The prince set the policy. Ritius had to enforce it. Rytius was a victim of this policy. How would a guided tour around their ancestral home change any aspect of any of this? Regardless of his brother's motivations in requesting it? Could it possibly matter what Ritius's motivations were? Rytius decided that it could have no bearing on anything else, and that it was thereby acceptable, even though he would have preferred not to have to deal with his brother at all. He marveled at how appropriate it was that he himself bore all these responsibilities—forgiveness and accommodation of family, obligations to colleagues, maintenance of personal boundaries and preservation of a way back for estranged relatives—while his brother bore nor acknowledged any save loyalty to the prince.

"ok, brother. You have to admit your timing is atrocious." His brother blundered about like a monster in the dark.

"Sometimes we are brought together by misfortune," said Ritius.

"The same way we're driven apart," noted Rytius.

"Yeah, that's right."

◆ ◆ ◆

Rytius had redecorated the master bedroom to match the era in which the home was built. He had womb and egg chairs, a thin, tufted leather couch on a frame of steel, a glass table, floating atop an asymmetrical wooden support. A phonograph rested atop a long wooden sideboard, a pair of stereo speakers hidden within it.

He kept his most prestigious artifacts and documents there: his televisions, film projectors, media players—things that might be traded. It's not that the materials filling three of the four remaining bedrooms were less valuable, but that they were less likely to be held to be so. So the master bedroom contained many audio and video recordings, and many landmark historical periodical publications, and the glass display case contained trading cards, from Topps baseball to Wacky Packages and Garbage Pail Kids; there were such archaic board games as Candy Land, Hungry Hungry Hippos, Monopoly, Connect 4, Sorry!, and Scrabble; numerous varieties of Barbie, a full squad of GI Joes (including Cobra Commander and Storm Shadow), My Buddies and Teddies Ruxpin, and such WWF Wrestling Superstars as Hulk Hogan, Randy "Macho Man" Savage, Ric Flair, Junkyard Dog, Andre the Giant, and other heroes of the 1984–1986 seasons. He also had several Rubik's cubes, a Lite-Brite, and a Simon Says from 1979.

Ritius spent hardly any time there, but went into the adjoining room, the art room, which might have been his own bedroom had he or Rytius ever lived there when they were children. There were mass-market West African goddesses, 1930s movie poster silkscreens, jade Buddhas and bronze *trimurtis*, impressionist and high-modern prints, many smallish watercolors and oils by Klee, Grosz, Picasso, Bearden, Klimt, De Lempicka, Lawrence, and others, and Ritius lingered over the titles of the many, many books lining the ceiling-high shelves—Jaffé, *De Stijl, 1917–1931*; Henri de Toulouse Lautrec, *Toulouse Lautrec*; Sandler, *The Triumph of American Painting*; Mark Antliff, *Avant-Garde Fascism*; Youngna Kim, *20th Century Korean Art*; Allan Wingate, *The Temples of Angkor*; Camille Paglia, *Sex, Art, and American Culture*; Wieland Schmied, *Neue Sachlichkeit and German Realism of the Twenties*—whereas the tables were covered with oversized picture books and museum catalogues with beautiful covers, vivid volumes on the lives and works of olden artists—*Van*

Gogh: The Complete Life, Matisse on Art, The R. Crumb Coffee Table Art Book—and the movements with which they were affiliated, from the Ashcan School to Orphism and from Dada to something called *Der Blaue Reiter*.

They moved into the third room, devoted to the works in the social sciences, of which each seemed to believe that it belonged to one or another distinct field of inquiry, be it sociology, anthropology, political economy, economics, or political science.

"So, are they not distinct fields of inquiry?" his brother asked him.

"They use different tools to examine the same problem," Rytius answered. "The problem was always wealth and therefore power, and who has it and who doesn't."

"Some things never change," Ritius noted. "So, what do they say?"

"The olden ones? About power and wealth?" Rytius replied. "What do we say today?"

"That some have it and some don't," Ritius answered.

"Why?" Rytius asked.

"That's just the way it is," Ritius said, blinking.

"The olden ones started with reasons why that is the way it is, upon which they disagreed," Rytius said. "So they said many different things. But different methods produce different answers, so the question was never honestly engaged in any case. The question was posed only during times of war or revolution, and most thinkers seem to have conspired to submerge it as soon as possible afterward."

"That seems impossible or overstated. How could such a conspiracy occur?" Ritius asked.

"Behind the backs of the conspirators," Rytius answered. "Advocates of this or that reason were able to hide behind a political-science methodology here, and pretend not to understand arguments from the econometricians, who pretended not to understand what political economists argued, while everyone ignored the historians, and on and on in circles forever. And so most came to agree with you, that there is no reason, their methods having precluded its finding."

Ritius turned his head and his entire body sideways so that he could more easily scan a row of titles—Adam Smith, *The Wealth of Nations*;

Bukharin, *Economic Theory of the Leisure Class*; Schumpeter, *History of Economic Analysis*; Lyn Marcus, *Dialectical Economics*; O'Connor, *The Fiscal Crisis of the State*; Marcus Noland, *Avoiding the Apocalypse: The Future of the Two Koreas*; Harold Robbins, *Fictive Capital and Fictive Profit*; Krooss and Blynn, *A History of Financial Intermediaries*; T.R. Malthus, *An Essay on the Principle of Population*; McCormack, The Emptiness of Japanese Affluence; Preobrazhensky, *The New Economics*; Benjamin Yang, *Deng: A Political Biography*; Marshall Sahlins, *Stone Age Economics*. "I've not read as much as you, but it seems safe to say that olden politics was entirely about economics."

"Theoretically, entirely," Rytius agreed, and led them into the fourth room. "The only distinctions I respect are among the practitioners," Rytius answered, waving at the wall of shelves to their left. "Political actors were quite a bit more forthright about their differences than the scholars." Ritius took it in. Isaac Deutscher, *The Prophet Outcast: Trotsky: 1929–1940*; Isaac Deutscher, *The Prophet Armed: Trotsky: 1921–1929*; John Reed, *Ten Days That Shook the World*; Jean Barrot and Denis Authier, *La Gauche Communiste en Allemagne, 1918–1921*; Facing Reality, *Facing Reality*; CLR James, *American Civilization*; CLR James, *State Capitalism and World Revolution*; *Situationist International Anthology*; Seymour Melman, *The Permanent War Economy*; Michel & Shakeed, *The Complete Guide to a Successful Leveraged Buyout*; Rudolf Hilferding, *Das Finanzkapital I*; James Scott, *Seeing Like a State*; Amadeo Bordiga, *Proprietá e Capitale*; Jane Jacobs, *Dark Age Ahead*; Susan Woodward, *Socialist Unemployment*; Tiffany, *The Decline of American Steel*; Marvin Harris, *America Now*; Marvin Harris, *Why Nothing Works*.

"The titles alone are an education," Ritius acknowledged.

"Yes, but if there's only one question, and if it is never clearly posed, then one can't follow the debate per se. One is forced to investigate the history of the question itself," Rytius answered.

"A higher level of abstraction," Ritius agreed.

"Which is why a lot of the titles in here are philosophical texts," Rytius concluded. There were rows and rows of books collecting the works of Hegel, Kant, Benjamin, Heidegger, Lukacs, and Adorno, and multiple translations and commentaries on them, and another entire shelf of the works of Marx and Engels and their many commentators, also in multiple languages. There were thousands of others, and Ritius seemed to be enjoying himself—Russell Jacoby, *The Last Intellectuals*; William James, *Pragmatism: The Meaning of Truth*; Gerard Helferich, *Humboldt's Cosmos*; Marcus du Sautoy, *The Music of the Primes*; Jean Charon, *Cosmology*; Eli Maor, *To Infinity and Beyond*; Franz Boas, *Race, Language and Culture*; Joseph Campbell, *The Mythic Image*; David Lewis, *We, The Navigators: The Ancient Art of Landfinding in the Pacific*.

Rytius let his brother explore. He forbade himself from speaking further and from hoping anything at all. Ritius stood straight, and appeared to have satisfied his curiosity.

"Have you read all these?" Ritius asked him.

"Of course not," Rytius asked.

"Why not?" Ritius asked again.

"It's mostly a matter of time, I suppose," Rytius went on. "We… I… we can't—everything is not equally accessible. Some of these works require a specific education, and it's not clear how to get it. So I… we just do what we can, and try to build knowledge and understanding."

"Perhaps if all the records were gathered together in one place," Ritius started.

"The records being in the same place has nothing to do with any-thing," Rytius interrupted, as rudely as possible. His brother had no reason to pretend, and yet his brother had indeed chosen to utter the prince's oily lies, as though they might actually persuade Rytius. It was two insults wrapped in a betrayal, when the betrayal alone would have sufficed. "We recordkeepers still have to do the work to make sense of them. Does the prince plan to support our work?" Rytius discov-ered that he had been hoping after all, that his brother would treat him with respect while doing his destructive duty. That he did not conveyed the message that nothing said had mattered at all to Ritius. He had no reasons of his own, and was somehow satisfied to have made himself entirely the agent of a spiteful and lawless power.

"I believe maintenance and storage to be support," Ritius said stonily, meeting his brother's gaze. There was nothing else Rytius could do. There was nothing more that he could hope from his brother, and he feared that there was no way ever to communicate with him again.

"It's theft," Rytius said. He was chilled by the finality of the rupture between them. He did not care whether his brother felt the same.

"It is the prince's lawful command," Ritius replied.

"And if we protest?" Rytius asked, curious to know the shape of the cage. He suddenly remembered that he had not gotten to any of the list of questions he had promised to ask.

"How exactly? I don't know what penalties the prince would impose, but you know the things that can happen."

"I don't know how we would protest," Rytius continued. "People find ways to express their displeasure."

"Brother, there's no need to make this any more difficult than it has to be," Ritius said. "Should I be concerned about you?" Ritius asked. He looked as though he might actually be concerned.

Rytius ignored him. "You're talking about the dispossession of immeasurable wealth."

"I don't know what you mean," Ritius said.

"We've devoted our lives to recordkeeping."

"There are no proposed rules against recordkeeping."

"You're being obtuse."

Ritius then chuckled like a slick child about to escape punishment on a technicality. "Perhaps *you* prefer a pillar of *fire* to a tower of records."

Rytius's face became a stone mask as his anger rose, and then he was ashamed at having identified the location of the nearest blade to hand, in his mind—the sixteenth-century rondel dagger in the art room—as Ritius vaguely threatened him. "It's not like that, brother, but it could be."

Ritius stood stock still. They were alone together in what should have been their childhood home. Rytius lived among the legends of their ancestors, and he felt himself to be new wine poured into the old skins of their family history, as though a new spirit would vivify the dust of their past, known and lost, and that he would re-embody the best of their bloodline. Ritius visited this home occasionally, to water their legacy with the blood of fresh battles and civic triumphs, feeling himself fully in the line, and wondering why his brother didn't see this clearly. He had wanted nothing more than to follow in his brother's footsteps, and it crushed him when his brother left the service. He never looked back. It was as though he had forgotten himself and their legacy entirely. As though perhaps with years of dedication to the prince they had sworn to serve with their lives for their lives he would or could show Rytius where he went wrong. Ritius never let himself think about nor wonder about his brother's persistence and steadfastness in his new course of life. What would make a warrior stand so strongly against his own legacy? The history of his own blood? The glory of his own battles? What would make a warrior leave the battlefield? Abandon all glower?

There are secrets these warriors keep from themselves. When a man goes to move the line of ultimate concern, he is never certain of his judgment. This necessary uncertainty is the cost of living a spiritual life. That is why such ways of life emphasize discipline, which is a method to keep one's soul safe, free of corruption, streamlined, unbound to anything other than the object of devotion. If the warrior has been disciplined, he can trust himself, and he can leap, knowing that he has not lost his way.

But warriors do lose their way. It is entirely a matter of discipline or, more precise, self-deception as to lapses in it. The conscience can be seared, the moral sense crazed, prayers can turn special pleadings, and instead of communion with the absolute, soundings of self-pity or self-aggrandizement. One constantly checks one's object of devotion against one's honor, but what if one's sense of honor is distorted? This is why there are regal, aristocratic, chivalric, clerical, republican, and democratic traditions. They show us the best that has been thought and done in these ways of life. And they, too, are subject to history, which means that they too can be lost. When confused, the warrior should look closely at this, his born or bred sense of honor. Self-deception is the subtlest corruption.

Ritius believed in that moment both that his brother was a fool for having lost his way, and that his brother was confused, having lost his way. He was sad on one score and scornful on the other. And yet he was not inflamed on behalf of the prince here. He did not feel the power of the state behind him, here before the fire crackling in the den. He still loved his brother, and were he quite a bit less serious a person, it would have been the perfect time for him to pat himself on the back, gratified that he himself was proving to be more mature than his own big brother. But he knew that Rytius felt himself in the service of principles greater than princes. If the world itself had not convinced Rytius of his error, what remained for Ritius to do? No, he had decided long before never to beat his head against that particular wall. And they shared quite a bit in common anyway. He had always admired Rytius for being so consistent, persistent, and insistent.

"Never change, brother," Ritius told Rytius.

"ok," Rytius answered. He was determined to be responsible to his colleagues, to ask their questions, and he therefore continued to speak with his brother. "I still want to know what this is all about. Why can't we just keep doing what we've been doing? If Feelharmonica wants to get involved with recordkeeping, he could give us a building, or fund our work."

"How would you like to tell him your concerns yourself?"

"If I wanted to do that, I would have done it already. I'm not going to sit in a room with that scoundrel and pretend to negotiate my own dispossession, or that of the others."

"Would you do so in public?"

"It's a public issue," Rytius noted. "Yes."

Ritius considered the range of options available to him. "The prince's council is set to meet this week Thursday. What about a public hearing with the council? It would be an opportunity for you to ask questions about the tower, and for the prince to answer them."

Rytius was momentarily pleased to have something to present his colleagues, until he realized that this was no favor, but just an opportunity for his concerns to be swept under the rug after a token airing of grievances. But with all the recordkeepers and as many interested citizens as they could gather, it was a chance to declare open conflict, and in such a state, anything can happen. So he asked whether "Feelharmonica himself is going to be there?"

"It's his council meeting," Ritius said.

"I gather the prince has some knowledge of recordkeeping if he's concerned about records," Rytius ventured. "Does he know anything about our game?"

"Only the barest notion," Ritius answered.

"I think a demonstration would be best," Rytius said. "It would allow me to communicate our concerns more effectively. Form and content, you know."

Ritius agreed, the brothers dapped, and Ritius departed.

Tent Raiders

That evening there was no game, but a presentation. It wasn't historical but contemporary. It wasn't high art or really even pop. It was something like *samizdat*, readymades, or early hip-hop. Fila had all the gear: the playback machines, the recorders, the cables, racks, and devices, all the screens for all the formats for all the sizes. Particularly late-twentieth-century mini-DV tape common in handheld videocameras from that era, of which there are many brands that are easy to maintain and that remain suitable for use.

The tapes are more expensive because the playing is the thing. Nobody is rushing out to buy a camera to record, because they don't have a clue what to do. But to *watch* something worthwhile? To *see* something everybody is talking about? You need to be part of a community something like that of the recordkeepers or you need your own copy. And that means you're at the mercy of the movie man.

Fila didn't like how it was one of the few occasions on which all the recordkeepers could get together anymore, even the Speculative Historians. There was nothing in the event itself to push them apart. *Showtime at Fila's Finds* was a tradition, and he promoted it with a poem, as a place where you might

> discover a discovery!
> no game but a frame to fall in
> to have a ball in
> to escape and go all in

Sometimes, understand, recordkeepers find things that are way out, unrelatable, perplexing and vexing, and they can't work it into a game because their referents are lame. Or, just the same, they don't know what to say about it. That's one way things can get into the show. There's a whole other way things can go.

◆ ◆ ◆

Dancy and Rob brought kettle corn. Voom made a sour-cream dip and a tomatillo salsa for his fried tortilla chips. GJ and Sugarpie had made one sweet-potato pie each, and they wanted everyone to judge which was better, because it was cinnamon versus cardamom. Floweria brought some yellow cake with real chocolate icing, made from real dark chocolate chips. D-Man said they were from Trinidad, because that's what the merchant told him. No, he didn't really have a reason to believe the man, but his great-great grandparents had been from Trinidad and he enjoyed imagining that tropical isle, a faraway place he would most likely never visit, and to which he would most likely never discover the substance of his connection.

"There's never not enough dessert," Fila noted. D-Man agreed, the reason being that he was working up an appetite moving folding chairs from the basement to the annex. He would have looked forward to rice and peas or red beans and rice or black eyed peas or fried chicken or a plate of crispy crawlers with shredded hash browns and ketchup or Sosoface was supposed to be helping, but he was flirting with Bonbon instead. Ice cream for dessert. D-Man wasn't mad at Sosoface. Not all the way. Fila wasn't as fast, but he couldn't be mad at that, either. D-Man had volunteered to help Fila, and that was that.

Fila had to get up and squeeze between the chairs that were set a little too close, even for this annex, which, while able to accommodate a hundred guests milling about on foot, what with all the distance and space in and among the shelves and racks of books and artifacts, could hold maybe only about 2 or 3 dozen chairs lined up in such a way that they all faced the same way, with a line of sight to the projector screen. All this in order to start the film. Consider the hieroglyphic language of twentieth-century electronics, high technology mass-manufactured consumer goods made in Asia, where the human languages are non-alphabetical, ideographic, tonal, and altogether inaccessible to the other major marketplaces. An international system of symbols, a pictorial pidgin, arose after the Second World War, and all pidgins are commercial trading languages. Like any language, it takes time to learn. The olden ones may have learnt it easier, given that they swam in such rich streams of commodities produced by a world working class across a global network of production and exchange. Language learning is always a matter of exposure. But that's why Fila had to be the one to press ▶ on the mini-DV camera.

◆ ◆ ◆

The picture was fuzzy like they usually were; folks don't clean the lenses of their cameras, dust gets into the sensor, pixels die. Handheld anti-jitter technology was in its infancy in the late twentieth century, as the contemporary trend of found-footage horror films conveys. It could not possibly have served as a source of horror unless it were real and unavoidable in recordings. Imagine *The Blair Witch Project* in a world with anti-jitter software. It's impossible. Now imagine the late 1980s television show *Cops* with smooth tracking shots, on a Steadicam. Similarly outrageous, a formal incongruity, a paradox. That's why *Tent Raiders*, a crowd-sourced community project "broadcast" by a network of smugglers, pirates, and Illadelphians remained *vérité*, no matter how big it got, no matter how many tapes got sold. Think of something like *America's Funniest Home Videos* produced by a team of psychopathic war boys from *Mad Max: Fury Road*, and then consider the universe of scandals possible in the production and distribution of such an underground video series, filmed by perpetrators of piracy, rape and pillage in the very act of piracy, rape and pillage. And then consider the sort of scandal *impossible* in the production and distribution of the same, only via intimate personal transaction and word of mouth across the entire North American continent. The distributors always cut the rape scenes, and there were never any corpses onscreen. With that you may begin to understand the fascination the series held across all strata of twenty-second century North America, let alone among such sensitive cultural types as recordkeepers.

◆ ◆ ◆

Darkness and suddenly a green spotlight, but it wasn't a green spotlight but a night vision scope clicking on to reveal a literal tent—but a large one, like those housing small carnival attractions or Bedouin families—being surrounded by raiders, like a squad of paramilitaries on reconnaissance. They used hand signals to keep mostly quiet, and the more one watched *Tent Raiders* the more one got to know and understand who the perpetrators were. Hand signals are like gang signs, and most of the perpetrators used some flavor of Illadelphian signal. Even here, in South Dakota, where the tent being raided was a slow-moving section of a semi-nomadic colony on the move. Probably for food reasons, as one can imagine would be a problem out on the Great Plains during winter.

"The chatter over the radio makes it feel so real," Dancy said. The quiet the perps kept was mostly for dramatic effect.

"It is real," Liz said.

"You know what I mean," Dancy said.

The perps were as a matter of course quite heavily armed, and there was almost no chance that any normal civilian grouping would be able to match them in firepower. They never seemed to come across other gangs, perps, or mercenaries.

Slacker perps were visibly unprepared on screen, goggles off, headsets around their necks, standing lazily at ease around the tent; the cam perp filming in night vision crackled threats to shape up and they did. There was some grumbling over the air, and a long beep of censorship.

"What was that about already," Fila said.

"Yeah, nobody even did nothing yet," Liz said.

"It's probably you know what it is. They don't even let them say it," Voom noted.

"They're calling dibs on the women," Hunnybunny agreed.

The cam perp swirled his index finger around to rally the other perps. Half surrounded the tent and half invaded, weapons drawn. The cam perp led the breach, and, once inside, he gave a slow look around, so as to film everything and everyone before waking the victims. They were sleeping soundly. Then he told the men outside to let off some shots. Pandemonium broke out inside among what appeared to be two families, with two sets of parents and two sets of children. Screams of surprise and a man jumped up alarmed to trip over his pallet and land on his wife, who had been trying to run from out of a crawl. It was almost funny, and then the camera cut to a new scene.

"And on the girls," Vinilla said. Her daughter was asleep at home with her sister as sitter.

There was neither muss nor fuss in the next scene, which was entirely silent. The two bound and gagged men and a teenage boy were led out of the tent and sat down.

"Why do they cut the sound?" Fila asked. "They're selling horror, right? Why not give us what we paid for, so to speak."

Men outside the tent had already removed the property from inside the tent, and were already going through it, splitting it into two piles.

"I think it's against the law," D-Man said.

The males had not been sitting for a minute before the two adult women and three tweenage girls were led out of the tent, also bound and gagged, and placed forcefully on the ground near the males.

"What law?" Sugarpie asked.

"Yeah, there's no distribution company to charge with anything," said GJ.

One perp set the tent on fire, and cam perp examined the pile of belongings precious to the two families. "What law?" Fila repeated.

"I'm saying, though," Rob said. "There's nobody to charge."

"So why censor then?" Fila asked.

Cam perp wasn't very interested in the families' pile of belongings. He walked back over to the victims. He spoke something to them, causing one of the men to fall over, and the other jumped to his feet, whereupon another perp slammed a rifle butt into his solar plexus. He crumbled to the ground as well.

"We agree the Illadelphians organize all this, right? They do the perpetrating and the recording and the first distribution, right?"

Nobody had any doubt about that.

"It's organized crime showing the world that they rule the world with vicious, inhuman brutality. And yet they are careful not to offend our sensibilities," Fila said.

"Like we can trust them, even though they are raping and killing and destroying. Like we can trust them not to...offend us, or something," Dancy agreed.

"It's propaganda," said Sosoface.

"Yeah, but how and what kind?" asked Rob.

Cam perp went back to the piles of precious belongings, those things these families troubled themselves to carry through the blizzards of their travels, and set fire to the larger, presumably the discard pile. He appeared to laugh with the perp who had been doing the sorting. Then he lit the other pile on fire as well.

"You can watch it with your whole family," Floweria said.

"Yeah. Only grown-ups get the whole show. But the essential part, that they rule the world with brutality and impunity, is a lesson for the whole family," Fila agreed.

Cam perp got close in on the victims while another perp forced them to watch their belongings burn. After all that, they weren't even victims of robbery, the *raison d'être* of the show.

"Train up a child in the way he should go, and when he is old, he will not depart from it," Fila concluded the presentation, and hit ■.

Madness

"Did you try the sweet potato pies?" GJ asked Voom, who was chatting with Dancy and Liz in the doorway. GJ was sure Voom had a crush on Dancy.

"I did," Voom replied, smiling. "Both of them, like Sugarpie said."

"Well, don't be shy. Which one did you like the best?" GJ asked.

"I preferred the one with the pumpkin spice," Voom said.

"Ain't no such thing as pumpkin spice," said GJ, sort of chuckling. He pulled from his shirt pocket the joint he had made that morning. He held it up as if to ask those gathered whether they would like to share it with him.

"Heck yeah," said Voom, nodding yes to the joint.

"You just mean the one that tastes like pumpkin pie," Dancy suggested to Voom. "Right?"

"But it's sweet potato, though!" chirped Liz. GJ was sure that Liz had a crush on Voom.

"That's right," said Voom, answering Dancy. "I know what it tastes like, but not what goes in it."

"What kind is it?" Dancy asked GJ, changing the subject. "You always have the best stuff."

"They be growing heirloom strains and ancient seeds and stuff, like spelt and rainbow corn," agreed Liz.

"I think they called it maize? excuse you?" Dancy smirked.

"Frickin'…millet," said Voom.

"Egads, I do believe it's emmer," laughed Liz, continuing Voom's construction.

"Fuckin'…fonio," GJ drawled, chuckling lightly. They all laughed. He lit the joint, pulled and exhaled a pungent cloud among them. "This," he coughed, "and I am pleased to present it, is Toe Jam."

"You ain't lying," Liz's eyes watered as she attempted to unstank her face.

"Oh my God, that smells awful," Dancy agreed, wincing.

"Like moldy lemon peels," said Voom, taking the joint.

"Yes!" GJ agreed emphatically. "But it tastes like…like chocolate…"

"Yogurt," said Voom, coughing. "Chocolate yogurt. A strange mix, with a strange aftertaste. Rich and smooth but tangy and acidic."

Dancy had to try it. "Oh, I see what you mean," she said. "The aftertaste is like…like lemonade or, um, lemon…"

"Ice cream!" coughed Liz, having taken the joint, pulled deeply, and held her breath. "Or key lime pie…" She looked up at Voom. "With pumpkin spice," she added, blinking suggestively.

GJ giggled as she passed him the joint again.

"Still smells like feet," Voom reasserted.

"Sweaty running shoe sock feet," Dancy said, crinkling up her nose. Voom grinned, pleased with her amplification. Sugarpie joined them just then, standing beside GJ, who put an arm around her waist and took a second pull on the joint before passing it to her.

"So whose pie did y'all like the best?" Sugarpie asked, embedding herself in GJ's arms and jabbing the air with the joint like eeny-meeny-miny-mo.

"They won't give me a straight answer," said GJ. Then he almost doubled over, giggling, pushing Sugarpie away. "Voom keeps talking like somebody ground up some pumpkins and made spice out of 'em."

"Aw, man, you're just giving me grief," Voom chuckled. "I just don't know which one was which, so I called it by the taste. The classic, traditional one. You know, the one that tastes like pumpkin pie."

"OK, cinnamon," Sugarpie agreed, nodding. "I told you they'd like mine better," she teased GJ.

"All's I'm saying is there ain't no such thing as pumpkin spice, and even if there was you can't refer to a sweet potato pie by calling it a pumpkin anything," GJ stated calmly, as though he were concluding a presentation in the game.

Dancy snorted a laugh and said GJ was tripping, and Liz giggled, too, at his sudden change in demeanor. GJ grinned and passed the joint to Voom. "Yeah, well," Voom chuckled too, as GJ stifled a giggle and attempted to compose his face. GJ crossed his arms, and leaned back against the doorframe, as though he were done arguing and would now rest his case and his body against the doorframe. He missed—he wasn't square in front of it—so he slid off to the side of it, reached out with his left arm to grab it, and extended his right arm behind him to break his fall. He managed to catch himself before he ended up on the floor. Voom,

Liz, and Dancy guffawed, and Sugarpie covered her mouth laughing, while pulling her husband back up out of his half-fall.

"Yuk it up," he muttered, attempting to square himself again. "Go right ahead." He appeared hurt in his pride.

"Oh, don't be like that, baby," Sugarpie stifled her laughter and leaned against him for a kiss. He jumped back, and he was still off-balance, so he fell again, and he did not catch himself with his hand against the doorframe, though he did try to slide along the wall to slow himself. This produced a sort of rotation, so that he looked like a tree turning and falling down. He realized he could not brake his fall, so he yelled "Timber!" and landed on his right side, and he cracked up laughing, there, on the floor.

Voom bent over to help him up and GJ snapped at him. "Watch you don't draw back a stump," and Voom was shocked and Dancy and Liz stopped laughing and Sugarpie got down quick.

"Wait a minute, GJ, what's wrong?"

"I don't like pumpkin pie, and I never ate it," he said. Voom was stunned, Liz was gapemouthed, and Dancy was frozen, waiting to understand.

"OK, but what are you so upset about? It's just pie," Sugarpie said, concerned.

"You remember my great grandmother?" he asked Sugarpie as he tried to stand up. He fell back down and finally sat against the wall. "She was a snakebearer, too," he spat, looking up at Voom. "She made pumpkin pie," he said venomously.

"What is going on with you, GJ?" Sugarpie wailed. "Why are you talking to him like that?" She shot worried looks at Dancy, Liz, and Voom, each of whom was also perplexed.

"Shut up, woman! I'm trying to tell you something!" GJ shouted. Sugarpie jumped back and stood still. Liz bumped Dancy and whispered telling her to go get Rob or Rytius or D-Man or Fila or somebody, one of the men, and Dancy did, backing away horrified.

GJ tried again to get to his feet. "I never told you she was a witch, did I?" he asked Sugarpie. "She was. She used to keep this big black leather book full of potions, spells, brews, infusions and incantation." He noticed Dancy was gone. "You ain't getting none of that tonight, Voom," he laughed. "Or ever. You know they're getting married, right? Her and Rob? She just likes the attention, stupid. And here you come, like a little puppy dog jumping all up in her face, trying to get a lick." He giggled in Voom's face, and then he noted gravely, "Speaking of puppy dogs, you're one Snoopy-looking motherfucker too, ain't you?" He could hardly stop himself giggling, and so he was pushing himself against the wall so as not to fall again. "Tell him what's up, Liz," GJ winked big at her and laughed a loud snort.

"I don't know what's going on with you, man, but I think you might need to go home," Voom said. "Right?" he looked to Sugarpie for support. She didn't know exactly how to respond.

"Like I was saying, that snakebearing bitch was sure enough a witch. I know. I've seen the book. She passed it down to her daughter, and she passed it down to hers, and that's my very own mama."

"Wait a minute," snapped Sugarpie. "Are you talking about your mama's recipe book?"

Dancy returned with D-Man, who smoothly took up the spot next to GJ on the wall. "My man," GJ greeted him, and tried to give him a pound, but it ended up being a back slap and a low five. "I'm speaking on curses," GJ declared. "In curses, as verses." He laughed sharply at his rhyme and glared at Sugarpie and Liz and warned them, "Don't think I don't see what's going on here, by the way. You sent Dancy to go get somebody to cool me out, and that's my main man and it's not just recipes. That's just what it *looks like*. The shit gets inherited."

GJ had managed to pull himself up fully erect, still against the wall.

"It's in the blood now. And it looks like a recipe book because it's all food potions, like pumpkin pie. And what is food? Food is nourishment. Nourishment for the body. But the soul can't live without the body. So food nurtures the soul as well. And so if you poison the body, you can poison the soul," GJ explained. He was calm. "It's witchcraft, plain and simple." D-Man looked at Sugarpie for an indication of what to do, and Liz and Voom were just as confused as Sugarpie was.

"That's what drug addiction is. Right? Loss of the soul via ingestion. Digestion. So if you curse the nourishment, that's not just any old curse. You're planting the evil deep down in the metabolic process, the hormonal regulation, the growth cycle of the individual organism, and that's a curse on all the future generations. The recipe is the transmitter, the information, the DNA, how it spreads," GJ went on. He was making a strained sort of sense, which made things somehow worse.

"And get this: it looks like culture. It looks like a recipe book. It looks like a family heirloom. And so the curse affects the minds of those who inherit it, and it spreads out further and further, deeper into the collective soul. So I have to listen to a redheaded snakebearer telling me about pumpkin spice. Fila's right about family. Fuck family. And fuck snakebearing witch bitches, too, God damn it," GJ finished.

Sugarpie had had enough. "OK, GJ, I think it's time to go. You ready?" He said he didn't care and his pupils were wide open. She put an arm in his and started pulling him off the wall while D-Man put his arm under GJ's other arm. They got him off the wall that way, but his legs buckled after a couple of steps, and he pulled Sugarpie to the floor, while D-Man held the other arm up. Sugarpie was not strong enough to walk him out. Voom stepped in to provide support.

"I told you to back up off me, you Red Baron Flying Ace–looking motherfucker!" GJ shouted, slapping Voom's hand away and wrenching himself from D-Man's grip. "You Samhain-dancing triplane-flying Grand Pumpkin–eating snake motherfucker!" GJ was on his own two feet, though falling forward again as he swung his right arm wildly wide, connecting firmly with Voom's left jaw.

Voom slumped to the floor and Liz shrieked and fell to attend to him while Dancy cried and Sugarpie yelled for help, and folks came running and D-Man grabbed GJ in a bear hug while Rytius and Sosoface held his legs to stop him kicking, and they carried him, laughing and crying hysterically, out of Fila's Finds.

The Castle Doctrine

It is well established that there was a time and place in the olden United States when it behooved every man to walk about armed. This was, in fact, a marker of manhood, and there were those forcibly excluded from it. Those who refused this blackmail of honor were not punished except by those who would then successfully abuse them, but they were subtly scorned. This was especially the case in the western territories after the Civil War, when men from the eastern and middle western states went out ahead of their families to establish homesteads and claim their piece of the lands then offered by the United States government, should the settlers subdue it. Including the antebellum South, more than half of the country was pacified by hard men such as these, who crafted a civics of menace, and a corresponding interpersonal ethics of threat. Both are well ramified, and there are higher orders akin to chess or speaking in drum.

It is for this reason that upon his return home that evening, Rytius showered for sobriety and descended to his basement, to collect materials for three improvised explosive devices with ballistic payloads and one, larger, with an incendiary payload. He reasoned to himself that his ancestral home was not worth much if his own brother would steal from within it that which made it important. What value was a property here in New Ark, where the prince would have it done?

The state and its laws may be arranged in such a way that the prince is authorized to act outside of the law. But this does not mean that their victims must act without benefit of the law their rulers abandon. Let them suffer a man defending his home and property. Rytius was determined that they would, and so he carefully spoon-sifted black powder into three tubes of cardboard, the first two about 6 inches long and 1 1/2 inches in diameter, and the last about 8" × 2". He held the first cardboard tube in place at the wide mouth of a glass quart bottle as he shook in the ball bearings and wood screws and bolts and washers. He made another like that, and for the incendiary he made a gallon of sticky fire, and loaded it with the third powder tube into an ancient plastic water jug. He set the incendiary device just inside the door of the master bedroom, the first room of his shop, on the second floor, while he set the two shrapnel devices inside the front door of the house, and just inside the backyard entrance to the kitchen. He set tripwires to trigger their electric fuses, but he left the circuits open, because he needed a good night's sleep, and he didn't want to worry about whether he would remember that he planted bombs throughout his home in the morning. One never knows exactly what to expect from a hangover.

Duck Eggs

Wednesday, February 6, 2143

The ducks honked and screamed Rytius awake from his nightmare of a pumpkin eating his hand as he attempted to light the candle in its belly. The lightbulb in his closet flickered and dimmed as he dressed, and so he hurried outside to see what the matter could be. The pen was flooded, and the hens were mad because they could not protect their eggs from the cold. The brook behind the house had overflowed its modest bounds and strengthened sufficiently to carry refuse from the Brookside market upstream, and so the rotten wood of a old, broken milk crate had jammed the paddle blades of his ginny. The twisted wire frame of the crate was intact and only slightly deformed, but its deformation had been sufficient to break the single plank of decaying, discolored wood that it had retained, which then crumbled and slid out of the mechanical tension grip of the frame. Rytius hardly touched the moldy board jamming the paddle before it disintegrated. The wire frame of the crate was set against the brook like the fish trap had been set against the Watsessing at Soverel Park, and Rytius observed how the flow into the box cut waves and ripples on the surface, which were then cut again, by identical wires, upon flowing out—squaring the modulation of the fluid, flowing back into itself.

He had to lift the pen up with his back to push a pair of bricks underneath its stilts, to drain it and to ensure that it remained draining. He told himself that the ducks might find the tilt engaging as he screwed the door hinge back into place, so that it would close correctly against the wind and rain, and he did not fail to collect the eggs, not only for his breakfast but also for the selling.

He had no idea what game he would play for the council, though he knew what his subject would be. It was too large. He worried, but not much, as he prepared a *huevo ranchero* of a single fried duck egg, a reskilleted piece of bacon, chopped in the pan, there, mixed with the egg, now a scramble, and some sort of greenery, and he chose some parsley from the icebox, washed it inadequately, he knew, and prepared himself for some grains of sandy soil. He didn't even chop it as much as he had chopped the bacon, but he rationalized this half-taken half measure as too minor to matter, because his teeth would do the work his hands hadn't. He *would* do the work, and not in the sense of taking it up to do it, but rather that in one way or another, the need satisfied by the work was so necessary to his being that it was thrust upon him every moment of every day. A living human requires to participate in human metabolic processes. As soon as a child is born, those processes are social. And so we grow.

Rytius ate quickly. He finished dressing, packed some drawing materials, and, remembering his binoculars, armed himself in a rare manner, with some dusty fiberglass body armor and a matching pair of six guns.

Public

Rytius arrived 90 minutes before the allotted time and posted up on the roof of the apartment complex opposite New Ark Center, from which he could observe the councilors and citizens as they walked past the Hall of Truth, the main space of what was formerly a multipurpose exhibition center, and into the Theater of Victory. The apartment building used to be a hotel, which meant that a sort of servile subterfuge was built into its form, an entire complex of service stairs and elevators hidden and made precisely inconvenient for residents.

There were 8 councilors for the governance of New Ark, and they did not meet regularly, because they did not need to. Most were sycophants, and their portfolios rarely required actual competence, as they were politically minded delegators of genuine tasks to properly constrained underlings. Treasure, Construction, Water, Power, Food, Trade, Law, and War. War Councilor Saberman Hawkins (the once-famed defector from New York, where he had served as Worrus Fish's Undersecretary of Defense) entered with Law Councilor Justice Boniface, and that was nothing out of the ordinary. Amfibean Brady, the engineer charged with Power, was the only other serious person—a legitimate scientist and inventor, who had attended several games in years past—but his competence served him only in the field or laboratory. Rytius watched them as they entered the hall, in their trains of advisers, bodyguards, and minders, hoping to discern either strange combination or schism, but he did not.

He waited there on the roof until the prince arrived. He had identified no surveillance to have countered. Upon crossing the street, he greeted some of the citizen stragglers entering the hall, and strode forth just as he was beckoned to do so, appearing to move at a moment's command. This greatly pleased the council and the prince.

"Play your game," Councilor Justice Boniface encouraged him.

Rytius walked to the center of the floor, facing the audience, backed by the councilors, who were also elevated.

He still had no idea what to say. He reminded himself to talk loud.

" 'It's a tough nut to crack.' No, no, that won't work. How about, 'it's a tough knot to untie.' That hardly rolls off the tongue slippingly," he mugged, mock-slipping while pacing back and forth across the floor.

"ᴏᴋ, one more attempt; how about 'it's a tough knot to slip.' That's good, right? I got the noose in and everything. It works, right? Good?" Rytius genuinely asked the audience for an answer. He got a hesitant, mumbled assent.

"ᴏᴋ, nice. I'm glad you agree. But you have some sort of idea of what good is after only two cases?" Rytius asked. The silence he required fell immediately. That's when he knew that he could play well with those gathered.

"All we had was a nut and a knot," he said, still pacing, and looking sternly at the listeners in the front row, before stopping and throwing his hands up to say, "Look, if it's alright with you, it's alright with me!" Rytius paused while they laughed.

"I didn't want to tell you all yet, but, er…" He paused again and the laughter built in anticipation. "I know all about nuts and knots," he winked. "Believe me." Rytius then performed an exquisite pantomime of autoerotic asphyxiation in which it was clear that the entire scene was an act of self-pleasure, and yet in which no particular motion or gesture appeared vulgar or lewd. As Rytius approached his fatal climax, an old man literally died in the aisle, and his people dragged him out, laughing. "ᴏᴋ, so you see that it doesn't take much to start playing. But that's damn near nothing. Nuts and knots. Both are essentially hollow. I mean, when we speak about them in anything other than a literal or a sexual sense, we mean that hollow, empty thing. It's either going to be empty because you need what's in it or it's going to be empty because you need to get out of it. But it's going to be empty. It's existence is a trip to nothing. It's a cipher. It's pure, evanescent form. Is it actually nothing?" Rytius paused and walked to the other end of the floor.

" 'How can you just play like that, from nothing?' " Rytius growled in a raspy voice. He paused and continued in his normal voice. "That's what this trumpeter from the olden days asked a younger piano player he was working with, because he was impressed at his improvisation. It wouldn't be long before a whole lot of people were, because he became widely known for being able to spontaneously compose entire musical structures on stage by himself on piano, in multiple styles and idioms. Others would transcribe his creations to later confirm his fidelity to the forms he played. Anyway, the young piano player's answer was, 'I just do it.'

"That's saying something. Let's not dismiss it as the arrogance of youth, but let's take it seriously. Let's run a little thought experiment in putting new wine into old bottles. I would take his answer, made in the twentieth century, and I say it in a spirit they didn't have back then. I'll say it like Fila would say it. Some of you were there yesterday, at his baby girl's naming. You'll remember what I'm talking about, and you'll know why I am saying it, and then I will explain to everyone how a new nut…I mean a new wine can fill an old sack. I'll explain it, because I don't want to fall into a trap I see set before me. Let me tell you what that trap is."

A murmur spread throughout the hall.

"We recordkeepers refer to ourselves as recordkeepers, and we have a relationship to ourselves such that we have never come to an agreement about what we're doing with our time. This means we have a conflicted relationship to ourselves, and at least two parts. The concrete fact is that there are two parts. My part believes it is the strongest and the best because we have discussed it among ourselves, I say, among those who think like ourselves, and we, those who think like us, have agreed upon a certain approach to our work. We preserve and document the past, and we spend our time investigating what the past was for those who lived it. We want to know the shape of their lives, the meaning they drew from their lives. The facts are important, but they are not the thing. We seek a higher-order knowledge of the shapes of relationships. Because if we know the shapes of the olden relationships, we can more easily see the shapes of our own. And *then*, and only then, can we use the facts, the details, for ourselves. Otherwise, we wouldn't know where to put them.

"It should be easier to relate to the past, but I don't need to tell you… We are children of oblivion, taking shelter amidst the wreckage of a continuity lost in an apocalypse we don't understand.

"And so we can't agree with those who don't think like us. They believe that they can trick the past into revealing the cause of the apocalypse. They confront the past as though it can be known directly, by asking it to disprove assertions, one at a time. It sounds elegant, like the scientific method, or a Socratic dialogue," Rytius paused and glanced briefly at the Councilor Justice. "Or a prosecutor's cross-examination. Each single assertion pulls in all the records relating to the assertion, and that sounds comprehensive, but by doing that it aligns those records to itself, ignoring their own inherent arrangement, let alone their relationships to records outside the scope of the assertion. Their work is negative, and while they pretend to eventually be able to derive positive knowledge from all this, in the meantime all they're doing is constructing a prism of exclusions, each one a new facet, making their view of the past that much more fractured and kaleidoscopic.

"They call themselves Speculative Historians. That's fine. If I had to state our differences plainly, with appropriate rancor on each side, I'd say we seek first ourselves to flourish, and they seek first our pasts to prune, as a precondition of flourishing. We are opposites, united in the same activity of research, debate, discussion, discovery, rediscovery, and I will credit them with the pursuit of knowledge.

"But what regulates our opposition? We haven't had debates on these matters in ten years, since 2133 when Fila Green and Tellem Ralph, the first two recordkeepers, split over the *Lancet*." Rytius paused to seek out their faces among the crowd. Tellem wore a benign smile and looked off into the distance, while Fila met his eyes, listening intently. "We clearly don't regulate it ourselves. We can't even agree to hold a debate to disagree. It's pretty sad, considering the stakes and the talent going to waste."

Some of the Speculative Historians muttered disapproval. Rytius understood. "Both sides believe the other to be wasting its talent and opportunity."

Rytius paused and walked over to the side of the stage, where he had lain his pack. He withdrew a wooden folding easel and a large pad of paper, and he spent several seconds setting them up in the center of the stage. The councilors could not see the paper.

"So, what regulates bodies united in opposition? If you were to poach an egg the whirlpool way, cracking the shell and dropping the egg into the vortex of a swirling bath of near-boiling water, you could see that the yolk and the white are held together by centripetal force, the force pulling inward in axial rotation. The medium and agent of that force is the hot swirling water bath itself. But it's not so obvious that there are two separate things going on at the same time."

He paused to draw it out.

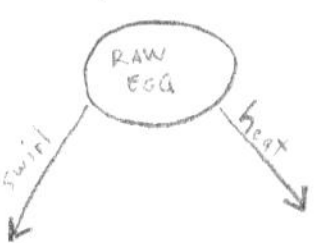

Rytius sighed. "I sure could use a hot, swirling water bath myself right about now," Rytius said, turning to look directly up at Councilor Justice Boniface, whereupon he danced toward her, lightly gyrating like a bachelorette party stripper, and pretended to seductively sponge-bathe himself through his body armor and leather coveralls—of which one strap was now unbuttoned and swinging to and fro—and his sweater and thermals. "Mm hmm," he moaned loudly.

Attendees wooed their disbelief and shock and fear.

She frowned and smiled at the same time, so Rytius turned back around to face the crowd, to waggle his eyebrows for a quick bit of comic relief. He turned back to her. "You can arrest me any old time you like," he said suggestively, presenting his arms for binding. "Do you, too, also like nuts and knots, as well?" There were more giggles and oohs. She smiled contemptuously and narrowed her eyes, as though to indicate that she had been a good sport but that gametime was now over. Rytius agreed, and turned back to face the public.

"But you know we've *been* in hot water," he said confidentially. There was no doubt that it was true, and those gathered vocalized their plain agreement.

Rytius paused and let his head fall back in exasperation, and then he let a deep sigh buzz his lips in exhalation. "These God damned princes," he moaned long and slow, dragging out the "-ces", as he turned around slowly to end his sibilation and rotation with gaze affixed on Feelharmonica, who neither squirmed nor bristled, though he shot Councilor Boniface a quick glance. Rytius tested Feelharmonica once more: "What? What?" He bucked up his chest and bounced around like a man pretending to prepare to fight. "If you're feeling froggy, jump!" Rytius froze in the stupidest threatful pose he could muster and looked menacingly at the prince with whom he had hunted pigeons and played tag long ago. He held it, and he held the prince's gaze until Feelharmonica cracked a crooked half-smile, and everyone laughed, and Rytius could go on, frog in hot water.

"Yes, the birth pangs of the Covenant of New Ark, the death throes of Prince Appall, the trilateral sibling rivalry we've got going on here, right, Feelharmonica? Mercs, taxes, shortages, rents, rants, rats, roaches, and ants.

"I think I can come right out and ethically propose to you that we should consider the whole of our society to be the swirling waters that regulate the contradictory unity of our little group. That might sound abstract or big, and it might be, but whatever it is, it's the opposite of profound. I want you to realize how mundane all this is.

"Nuts and knots. Something from nothing. New wine, old sacks. Frogs in swirling hot water baths. Centripetal force. A real situation. A conundrum. Reality." Rytius paced a bit.

"I still haven't decided the topic of my presentation, but I'll tell you when I'm finished." Everybody laughed, most applauded, and some recordkeepers stood to applaud.

"You know I'm just playing, though. It's all in the game. I know the prince, and I might maybe even say that I know him well, and, of course, my brother works for the prince. I know that the prince and his council work hard to ensure our means of survival, and I myself have personally fought and shed blood for New Ark's independence, for the prince's place at the table with the other rulers of these lands. So I know that when something needs doing, the council is on top of it." Rytius backed off to one side of the floor and turned to face the council, and he began to clap, and to lead those gathered in a round of grateful applause.

"And Prince Feelharmonica leads the council in virtually all matters. He delegates duties in a responsible fashion, but there must be no doubt that Prince Feelharmonica has agreed to any significant state action, policy, or regulation in New Ark. Am I right, councilors?" Rytius asked the councilors, who agreed, sensing some rhetorical danger, but not caring much one way or the other.

"So, in a very real sense, if something in society boils up to the level where it requires state intervention, it's coming under Feelharmonica's purview. As it should.

"So, we have demonstrated that Prince Feelharmonica, as sovereign of New Ark, is the master of all those processes that work on and about the bits of our lives. He is the poacher. I mean, he is—must be—the cook boiling the water, swirling it, and dropping the egg.

"And yes, that is true almost by construction, because of the manner in which the power of the sovereign flows through the law and the rest of the power sculpture. And we knew this even before this hearing began because we knew that Prince Feelharmonica's policy is the reason for the hearing at all."

Rytius paused to expand his diagram. "I want you all to remember that it's two things happening at the same time. If you just heat the egg, you get a boiled egg. If you just swirl the egg, you get some sort of raw egg soup."

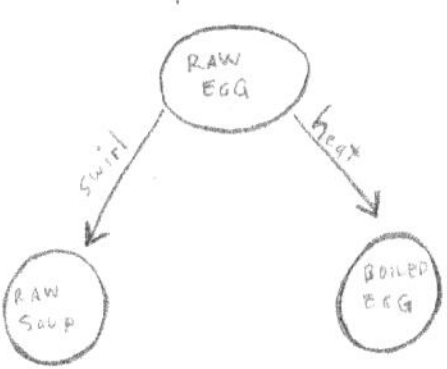

"The swirling hot water works *inside* the egg, too," Rytius began again. "There is a time, a window within which the two fluids held together in opposition can still slide apart if some small factor of rotation or temperature changes. The swirling water takes a different time to cook each fluid. It works from without by centripetal force, that's the law for instance. How does it work within? With heat. That's ambient radiation."

Rytius drew a poached egg by itself at the bottom of his diagram. "I didn't label the white, but you can see the yolk there."

"Do you guys know the joke about the fish in the water?" Rytius asked. Somebody yelled "Tell it." "Some of you might remember it from

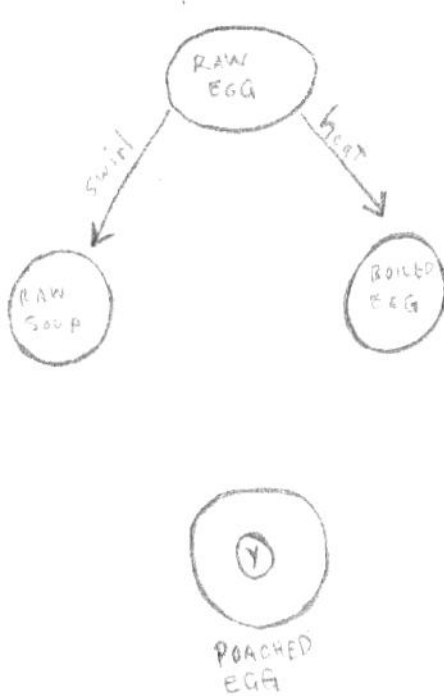

Rainbow's Pot O'Gold Get Down last year?" Rytius asked again. Some recordkeepers sounded their recollection.

"I'll tell everybody," Rytius said. "There are these two young fish swimming along, and they happen to meet an older fish swimming the other way, who nods at them and says, 'Morning, fish. How's the water?' The youngsters just ignore him and keep on swimming. A couple minutes later, one of them looks over at the other and asks, 'What the hell is water?'"

There was a nice round of laughter at the arrogance of youth.

"This is the joy of recordkeeping. You learn these little tricks like listening when people talk," Rytius laughed with the listeners. "What is it that you're surrounded by but just don't know? If you're a fish, it's water. If you're one of us, here, alive, today, in New Ark, it's hot water!"

The citizens laughed at a higher pitch, now anxious because implicated.

"Let me be honest with you about something. I just made a mistake and I'd like to apologize. I was demagogic and went for a cheap joke just a second ago, about the hot water. That just puts us right back where we started, and it makes me have wasted a good minute or so developing the theme of something in the hot ambient-radiation water.

"Because I'm embarrassed now, I'll just say plainly what I should have said, which is that we need to identify our water. In this particular case, the confiscation of the lifework of dozens of citizens of New Ark by Prince Feelharmonica himself. It's like a noose around our necks.

"But let's look closely, please, at our metaphor and our situation. We have an egg swirling in hot water, slippy for a time, and as the water transmits its heat to those two, they set, locking into their final positions against one another, defined by one another. They can no longer change form, though they can be broken apart. But you have to have both the heat and the swirl simultaneously. That's the only way to get to the poached egg."

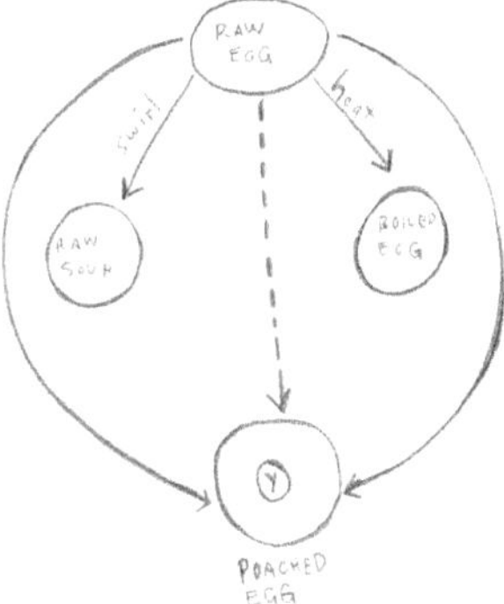

"And let's not forget that the heat and the swirl have to be coordinated, somehow, in their simultaneity. That's up to the cook, not to overheat the water, and not to swirl too hard."

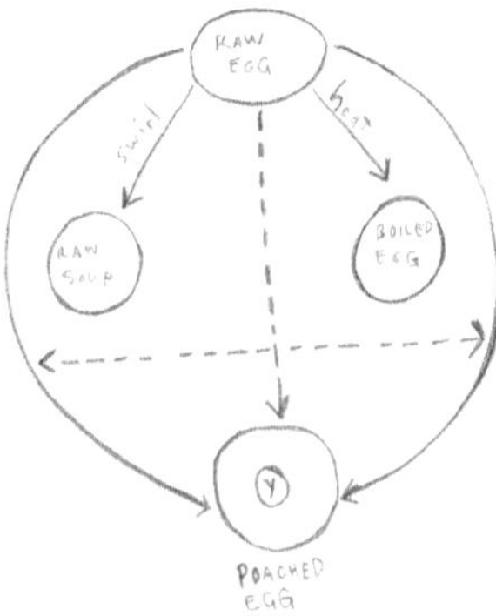

"By now most of you probably think that I am laying a foundation to accuse Prince Feelharmonica of meddling in the affairs of the record-keepers to the detriment of my faction and the benefit of the Speculative Historians. It's a much simpler matter than that, and it has everything to do with why our two factions could never come to terms with one another, why we never finished our debate, and why water is elemental, despite being a compound. Water is that which mixes the miscible. This can mix with that in the medium, and the medium is the water, which is the third element, and thereby always an element. That's logical.

"But in the real illogical world, some of the waters in which we swim are lax penalties for ignorance, open corruption in the production of wealth such that the people cannot pay even those paltry fees, and craven fear consumed as though it were respect. Can you imagine the fellows on the bed of this river?"

Rytius modified his diagram. "Remember, you can't unpoach an egg, and you can't cook an egg and then swirl it, or swirl it and then cook it. Poaching is a combination of the two, but you can't factor either one out and get to a poached egg."

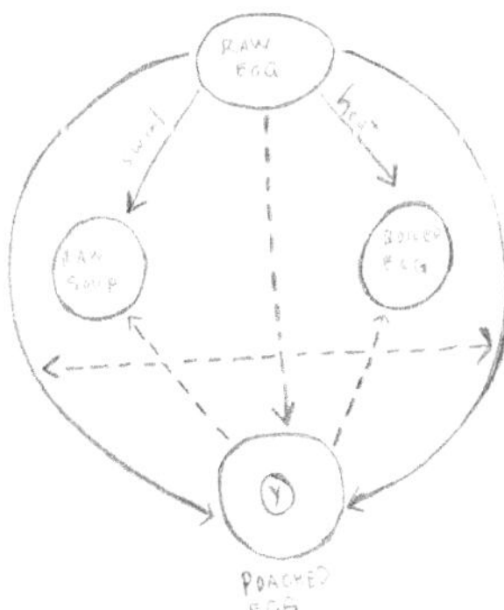

"But I'm trying to spark something here with these two concepts—the miscible mixing medium in which we swim and the swamp of corruption crawling with strange bedfellows. I'm trying to push them together and hopefully reveal the sort of waters in which, say, Prince Feelharmonica and any faction of recordkeepers could mingle. We're talking about swirling heat, cooking the inside an egg. It's no run-of-the-mill corruption, like money under the table, that sustains our little group, yolk and white, in disunion. It has to be more like the prince and the faction share a worldview. That's part of the coordination. They fit together in a way that escapes immediate understanding of either. Like water for the young fish.

"Even better, to keep the shapes aligned, it is more like…the ever more rigid, ever more opaque white of the egg is the way the water appears to the yolk. Tellem's faction is the way the whirlpool of corruption, i.e., our world, appears to us, the core group performing the core activity without which the faction wouldn't exist. While the prince's confiscation and this hearing are somehow a manner of regulation."

Rytius drew another diagram next to the first.

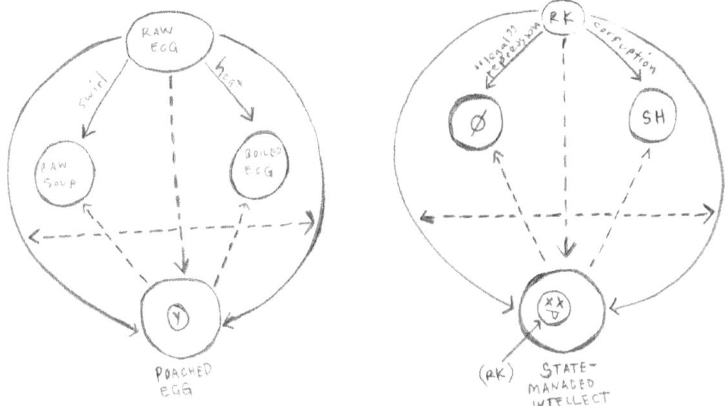

It was virtually identical.

"It's all about coordinating the processes. It stands to reason that there would be something on the order of collaboration between the prince and the Speculative Historians, to place them in control of the tower and its research objectives. My brother Ritius is charged with enforcing the law, such as it is. He has to press it home, and that's the swirl. But the corruption… The corruption is the law itself—the entire legal apparatus—and the agent of that corruption must be none other than Councilor Justice Boniface, administrator of that apparatus."

There were jeers from the Speculative Historians. Ritius, seated in the front row, gestured to a lieutenant, whereupon additional security personnel gathered at the exits. The hall was full of commotion. Tellem walked out, and Rytius breathed deeply and remained calm. He turned to face the council, and he made a point of meeting each of their eyes.

"Speculation?" he continued. "Yes. But I want you to see just how strong speculation can be."

"They swim in the same water. The prince feels himself adrift, and the Speculative Historians promise to be able to shout 'Land ahoy!' any day now, as they have for years. The prince wants a shrink-wrapped, prepackaged history, a usable past upon which to build his kingdom, and the Speculative Historians want to rediscover America, even at the cost of mistaking the natives for Indians. Again. This is the worldview they share. They both want firm ground to stand on. They are afraid of water.

"So, the trap I have to avoid today is saying anything to negatively influence the prince's decision. There's something else, too, for which I have already apologized.

"That's demagogy. See, I could been taking easy shots at our prince and his council the whole time, testing their patience, but meanwhile mastering the hall. But I want to fill old sacks with new wine, and that new wine is a new spirit abroad, and not just among us recordkeepers. Fila identified it yesterday for the first time, in the way we name our children.

"This is the *humility* we have learned in the loss of our past, and we should be grateful for it. The way we name our children shows that we know something the olden ones didn't: the relationships we build are more important than the ones we are born to. Or those we rediscover while seeking lost shores, magic treasures, or readymade narratives. Family names, and even family histories, are accidents. What we choose to make of ourselves in light of them is what matters. We know this. All of us who have chosen our names know this. We just don't know that

that's what we know.

"Well, now we know, and Fila said it first. I could keep this knowledge to myself, as I speak up here, and not let one half of the audience in on the secret I am sharing with the other half, so that the first half doesn't understand the passion of the response to arguments they mistakenly believe themselves to understand. This would disorient them, but they would feel the force of our side. I could master the hall that way, too. But the target is off. I don't want to persuade non-recordkeepers of anything other than the value of recordkeeping, and I want to valorize neither the hoarding of knowledge in secret nor the hoarders of secret knowledge.

"My only target is the nexus of corruption that brings us here today. And that nexus includes those I am still willing to call recordkeepers, though they themselves are not.

"I want to expose all of this. And I want you to see how funny it is, from my point of view, and then I'll close. Remember, the Speculative Historians are the form the state takes for us. The state is aligned with them, and the state may as well be them. Because the state has no special existence for us except through our relation with them. Which is how I solved their relationship in the hot water metaphor. And that's the only way I could sketch out the power sculpture, revealing the nature of the relationship.

"I want to confess one more instance of demagoguery. That's the metaphor of egg white and egg yolk taking their final form against one another, defined by one another. That's good as far as it goes, but it's not really applicable here, because we never excluded them because we could never agree to disagree. We could never really hash everything out. We were always fatally split, and, having failed to achieve the impossible, we recordkeepers, the only ones who actually ethically require the confrontation, are cursed that when we finally get it, it takes the form of us against what is, effectively, the world.

"So, in attempting to save my nuts by slipping the knot of the noose the prince has around our necks, I fell…no, it felt like I was falling, but I had always been sitting, like a frog, in the swirling hot whirlpool of corruption that is the sovereignty of New Ark, only there to discover, while dissolving into broth, that the swirl and the heat have killed once and for all any potential for life the egg may have had. That's the cooking metaphor, though, and the frog is done.

"I grab my nuts as the noose gets tighter, and I pray I can, one more time, Lord, pull something out of nothing. It better be good, and I hope they can tell after just one game.

"Before I close, with words of no particular fire, because I doused my own flame, I would like to say, in the language of the marketplace and the lawyers, and the lawyers of the marketplace and the marketplace of lawyers, that recordkeeping is a real value deal, I mean in terms of civic virtue. Consider that I just sketched the outline of an ongoing crime involving Prince Feelharmonica, Councilor Boniface, my brother, and Tellem Ralph. I don't have conclusive evidence, but you can see what's going on. Right? So, I'm saying, Prince, call me after you kick these scrubs to the curb, ок? We'll have lunch. My treat.

"My presentation tonight will have been about how to blow your game up in front of everybody but still come out on top because record-keeping has been real, folks."

Snake

Administrative staff and security personnel crowded the rear of the stage, and this made it difficult for a page to squeeze through; he was frisked twice before Ritius took note of him and pulled him aside. He leaned into Ritius's ear and said something that first angered and then amused Ritius and then it appeared to have been resolved, because Ritius went back to his conference with Feelharmonica, Boniface, and War Councilor Hawkins. Rytius suspected that his brother had received bad news about casualties sustained during a confiscation, which certainly should have been delayed pending resolution of the affair before the council. Ritius demilitarized the exits and left the building without saying goodbye, and Rytius was sad for the young men that he was now certain he had killed that afternoon.

Ritius learned that he perhaps should be wary of underestimating his brother as well.

Recommencation

The rain had stopped freezing because the drops were too large. There were no washerwomen washing nor fishermen fishing, because the rivers had risen past their banks, and the waters flowed over the footbridges. Ritius accompanied Prince Feelharmonica to the tower for an inspection, and the road up the mountain was treacherous, slick with loose mud from the earth moved for the tower's construction, and so the drivers drove slowly, and they were killed by long-distance snipers. The bodyguards rallied to defend their masters, but they were quickly dispatched, also from afar. Ritius and Feelharmonica exited their trucks with their arms raised for the captain of the assault team to lead them into a blasted cave nearby, where Prince Razorbeem awaited. He told Ritius that he wanted Ritius to watch and learn how a prince behaves. He had one of his men hold his brother's head out, pulling him by the top of his Afro, and then he asked his brother if he had any last words, and as his brother was preparing to deliver his last words, Razorbeem shot him in the back of the head, demolishing his face. He told Ritius that no warrior can live without a prince, and that Ritius sprouted too late, in the wrong place, only to be cut down, like a watermelon seedling in the middle of a lawn before mowing day. Ritius may have stood a chance had he tossed Razorbeem from the swing or the like before Razorbeem learned to speak. Consider that this motherfucker named himself some mean intimidating shit like Razorbeem at or around the age of 6. He led Ritius outside, and they walked to the tower structure, where his men tied Ritius to one of its beams. He had his men gut Ritius with their swords. They then set fire to the tower and the entire built near environs, whether tower or ruin or squatted domicile. The fires fought the waters, and the waters always win, but in a building, the fire can race ahead of the water, setting more aflame than is put out long enough to burn it down. That's what happened to the tower, and the electrical wires strung alongside it collapsed into the sloping canyon below, where they set fires to trash and trees and caused a three-car vehicle collision.

Razorbeem's crack squadron fled the scene while Razorbeem radioed his man at the Little Falls dam to loose the flood gathered since his lieutenant at Great Falls had done the same minutes before. That Little Dam lieutenant did so, and the sovereignty of New Ark was drowned in flood once more, its final oblivion. That flaming tower toppled into the Great Notch, and those wires sparked fires across the light forest there, which spread. The fires fought the waters, and the waters won.